MW01135788

HIGHLANDER UNRAVELED

Highland Bound Series

ELIZA KNIGHT

MORE BOOKS BY ELIZA KNIGHT

PRINCE CHARLIE'S REBELS

The Highlander Who Stole Christmas

Prince Charlie's Angels

The Rebel Wears Plaid
Truly Madly Plaid
You've Got Plaid

THE SUTHERLAND LEGACY

The Highlander's Gift
The Highlander's Quest
The Highlander's Stolen Bride
The Highlander's Hellion
The Highlander's Secret Vow
The Highlander's Enchantment

THE STOLEN BRIDE SERIES

The Highlander's Temptation
The Highlander's Reward
The Highlander's Conquest
The Highlander's Lady
The Highlander's Warrior Bride
The Highlander's Triumph
The Highlander's Sin
Wild Highland Mistletoe (a Stolen Bride winter novella)
The Highlander's Charm (a Stolen Bride novella)
A Kilted Christmas Wish – a contemporary Holiday spin-off
The Highlander's Surrender
The Highlander's Dare

THE CONQUERED BRIDE SERIES

Conquered by the Highlander
Seduced by the Laird
Taken by the Highlander (a Conquered bride novella)
Claimed by the Warrior
Stolen by the Laird
Protected by the Laird (a Conquered bride novella)
Guarded by the Warrior

THE MACDOUGALL LEGACY SERIES

Laird of Shadows
Laird of Twilight
Laird of Darkness

PIRATES OF BRITANNIA: DEVILS OF THE DEEP

Savage of the Sea
The Sea Devil
A Pirate's Bounty

THE THISTLES AND ROSES SERIES

Promise of a Knight
Eternally Bound
Breath from the Sea

THE HIGHLAND BOUND SERIES (EROTIC TIME-TRAVEL)

Behind the Plaid
Bared to the Laird
Dark Side of the Laird
Highlander's Touch
Highlander Undone
Highlander Unraveled

TOUCHSTONE NOVELLA SERIES

Highland Steam
Highland Brawn
Highland Tryst
Highland Heat

WICKED WOMEN

Her Desperate Gamble
Seducing the Sheriff
Kiss Me, Cowboy

☙❧

HISTORICAL FICTION

Coming soon!

The Little Mayfair Bookshop

TALES FROM THE TUDOR COURT

My Lady Viper
Prisoner of the Queen

ANCIENT HISTORICAL FICTION

A Day of Fire: a novel of Pompeii
A Year of Ravens: a novel of Boudica's Rebellion

FRENCH REVOLUTION

Ribbons of Scarlet: a novel of the French Revolution

SECOND EDITION
MARCH 2021

COPYRIGHT © 2016 ELIZA KNIGHT

Cover Design by Kimberly Killion @ The Killion Group, Inc.

Edited by Erica Monroe

For all of my wonderful readers. Every day I write is a joy because of you.

MOON MAGIC

BY ELIZA KNIGHT

When thunder crashes
And lightning illuminates
Magic comes to pass.

Thistles sway, dancing
Purple petals and green stems
So very lovely.

Rain falls in crystal torrents
Sparkling drops on fingertips
Liquid Sustenance.

Black clouds shield the sun
Blanketing the world in darkness
Taking away our sight.

The castle climbs high
Battlements touching the sky
Striking fear below.

Warriors come now
Their weapons shined and sharpened
Prepared for vengeance.

We will survive this
Surge of ruthless cruelty
For we are strong, wise.

Loneliness touches
Us all and can break hearts
Leaving us wretched.

Massaging the soul
Flexing your capacity
To accept love's hold.

Flames burst, destroying
Everything in its path
Poisoning, tainted.

The evils of men
Devastate the innocent
Obliterating.

Do not surrender
To one who strips you, attempts
To watch you bleed dry.

Fear paralyzes
Only those who allow it
Be strong, be steady.

Afraid of being
Broken leaves one hopeless and

The future stark, bleak.

When hope does soar high
So too does joy and pleasure
Fostering courage.

Brave and courageous
Forge ahead, part from the past
And tumbling forward.

Beneath moon magic,
Lovers' gentle strokes bring bliss
And sweet surrender.

A precious ending
A love that shan't be broken
By the bonds of time.

🦋 1 🦋

EMMA

Present Day
Drumnadrochit Village
Scottish Highlands

"Just where the hell have you been?"

I woke to the sound of Steven's berating voice pounding through my skull.

Wait—Steven?

No, no, no...

Blinking, I look up at the modern day ceiling. At the familiar water stain. Rusty-gray, and if I squinted my eyes, I could make out the shape of a rabbit in its pattern.

"Emma, goddammit, I'm talking to you."

I blinked again. Disbelieving what I saw, heard.

Modern ceiling. The one I stared at for several nights while on "vacation" with this man—because it wasn't what one would normally call a vacation. Only a moving of location. A place that was not my home. But the same old shit, the same nasty Steven.

My first husband.

"For fuck's sake, Emma! Why are you even dressed like that?" Steven shouted, his words sounding as though they came through a megaphone from a mile away. *Boom. Boom-boom.* His footsteps pounded on the floor, closing the minuscule distance between us and I tried not to flinch.

"Steven?" I asked, rolling my head to look over at him. I hoped by saying his name aloud this nightmare would disappear.

How was this possible?

How was I here?

It had been over two years since I'd left him, racing through a storm when lightning had struck. I'd been transported back in time to 1542, and into the arms of Logan Grant. My soul mate. My true husband.

The lump in my throat grew, but my mouth was dry. I couldn't swallow, only lay there, feeling my tongue grow thick.

Close enough now to touch me, Steven reached out and plucked none too tenderly at the arm of my gown.

My clothes were soaked through. A plain green gown. The wool scratched against my soggy skin. My linen chemise was tangled around my legs.

Why was I all wet? I closed my eyes listening for the sounds of a storm outside. I could hear the faint splatter of raindrops, not the torrential downpour kind, just a soft rain, one that turned into a mist.

"Are you going to answer me?" he shouted.

"What...?" My eyes popped open. I could barely get the word out. My mind whirled so fast nausea filled my belly. Was this a dream?

Or had my life with Logan been a dream?

Tears pricked my eyes.

Steven's fist slammed down on the bed beside me. "You have embarrassed me for the last time."

I flinched, wondering if the next slam of his fist would be on my body.

I couldn't speak. I didn't know what to say. How could I answer him? Did he even want to hear what I had to say? Quite frankly, I didn't give a shit.

"Did you know I was arrested? Do you even care?" he droned.

No. And No.

He let out a frustrated, animal-like growl. "I've been searching this godforsaken countryside for weeks. Trying to clear my name. They thought I murdered you. Half my business partners have dropped their contracts." He gave me such a hard stare, I was certain, now that he'd found me, he was considering murder.

"How... How long have I been gone?" I managed to ask, working to sit up.

"Three months." He shoved me back down.

Three months. That was *all* I was gone? And yet, years had passed with Logan. Years of love, of adventure, of hardship. I was a changed woman. In 1544, which was what it was when I left, I was strong, confident, happy. I was a mother.

Oh, dear God...

I pressed my hand to my middle, feeling the new squishiness of my belly, the place where my son had occupied just six weeks before. I swallowed hard. Trying hard not to cry. Praying Steven hadn't seen the way I touched my abdomen.

My baby...

An ache, deep and profound, filled my chest, suffused my bones.

How could this be happening?

Steven narrowed his eyes at me, scanning me from head to toe. "You look different. Fatter."

He sounded disgusted. But I knew it didn't matter how I looked, bone-thin or thick as a whale, he'd never be satisfied.

And, I *was* different. I had been proud of myself. Logan had loved me and called me beautiful every day. Yet, Steven had the power to strip away all the ways in which I'd changed, blossomed under Logan's love. I felt small, insignificant.

I curled up in a ball and rolled away from him, unable to look at his hateful face. Tears rolled from my eyes. I was powerless to stop them. I bit my knuckles to keep mournful sobs from leaping out of my mouth.

My true husband, my love, my child, my friends. My life.

All of it was stripped away from me.

In the blink of an eye.

Happiness, that had been mine, was gone.

Steven made a disgusted sound and headed for the door.

"We're going home, Emma. You're going to tell the authorities you ran off, but now you're back. You're going to pay for what you've done to me. I don't know how, but you will."

I didn't say anything. I couldn't even if I tried. No words would come except for Logan's name, and Saor, the name of our baby son—meaning free.

The door slammed closed and I jumped.

You're going to pay...

Steven's footsteps pounded down the stairs. I could hear him shouting at someone. Maybe his mother. But I didn't care. I wasn't going to stay here, and I wasn't going back to the U.S. with him either.

I wasn't going to *pay*.

Gathering a strength, which I didn't quite possess, I sat up on the springy bed and swiped at my tearful eyes.

I had to figure out a way to get home—to 1544.

Again.

Leaning on sheer will like a crutch, I shuffled toward the

window, peering out at the graying, cloud-filled sky. Rain wetted the street, making the asphalt look shiny black. Two elderly women walked arm and arm down the street; their heads bowed low, beige raincoats splattered with raindrops, a single black umbrella over their heads.

We'd vacationed in the summer. August I thought, but I couldn't quite remember. I'd worked so hard to forget my past. My life with Steven. I didn't want to remember. Didn't want to relive it. He'd been emotionally abusive to me. Crushing me from the inside. I'd sunk inside myself and become a shell of a human being. A stranger, even to me.

I clutched at my chest, feeling my heart race and ache.

It must be November now. Or close to it. In the U.S., families would be preparing to celebrate Thanksgiving. Buying turkeys, vegetables, looking up recipes and booking flights.

I never liked Thanksgiving. Not because I didn't like turkey or cranberry sauce. The holiday had always been oppressive in Steven's house. Not my house. His. And I had no family to celebrate with.

My mother-in-law would come over, a few of his other distant family members and business partners. Everyone would be kissing Steven's arse (*God I miss Logan*) hoping he'd cut them a slice of his multi-million dollar pie.

I shivered. A chill filled me all the way to the bone. An icy feeling that I knew wouldn't go away until I was in Logan's arms.

A soft knock sounded at the door. Not Steven. Nothing about him was soft, and he'd not knock anyway.

I didn't turn away from the window. Didn't beckon whomever it was to come in. I stood still, silent, hoping I could wish my way out of this room. Pinching myself and praying this was just a nightmare I'd wake from.

But I knew, deep down, that this was real. I was awake. I was back in present day.

My life with Logan had been real, why else would my full breasts ache with the need to feed my child?

"Mrs. Gordon?" Mrs. Lamb said from the other side of the door. Her voice sounded far off. Older.

I still didn't answer, but I could hear the handle jiggle and the creak of the door as she pushed it open.

I looked down to my feet, muddy and barefoot. Where had Steven found me? Or had I just appeared here? I didn't remember walking through the mud.

"Are ye all right, dear?" she asked, also staring at my muddy feet.

I pressed my lips together, gritted my teeth. Shook my head, and water droplets pinged against my face. Mrs. Lamb had helped me to escape the last time. I owed my new life to her.

"I brought ye a tea."

I didn't want tea. I *wanted* my husband. My child.

"No, thank you." The words came out harsh, bitter, and I was immediately contrite. She didn't deserve my anger. It wasn't her fault that Fate had brought me back.

She pressed forward, her feet skimming softly over the rug I'd muddied.

"Drink, dear. It'll make ye feel better."

I glanced down at the older woman; her arthritic fingers curled on my shoulder, a teacup and saucer jiggling in her other hand. I took the cup, not because I wanted to drink it, but because I was afraid she'd drop it.

"If ye want to talk..." she started, but I cut her off.

"I'll be fine. And I never got to thank you—before."

She shook her head. "I can't help feeling..."

"It's not your fault I'm back," I said, my voice sounding hollow without emotion. "I have no idea why I'm back."

I was flat. Numb.

Mrs. Lamb shook her head again. "But if I'd—"

"You set me free," I whispered. I felt my womb lurch and the tears that I'd managed to quiet, once more stirred behind my eyes.

"And yet ye are back." She sounded confused.

I nodded, though in my head, I swore, I was not going to be back for long. "Not of my choosing," I said softly.

"I'll help ye again, lass." Mrs. Lamb backed out of the room, and once she'd closed the door, I set the cup down on the dresser, my heart pounding.

I couldn't wait for her to return. I had to leave. My limbs buzzed, my heart raced and my mind was a jumble of panic.

I yanked at the lock on the window, praying that it would unhinge. God, why wouldn't it budge?

When was the last time someone had opened it?

I tugged and tugged and tugged.

Finally it wrenched free with a loud, metal on metal grating sound. I flung the window open; not daring to look behind me, afraid that Steven was going to come through the door at any moment, jerking me back into his life.

How could this have happened? The question repeated in my mind over and over like a bad song I couldn't flush out.

Why did Fate decide I could no longer be with Logan?

What had I done?

I stuck my leg out of the window, the water on the outside of the windowsill making me slip slightly. I was weak. Limbs shaking. Fingers trembling.

But I wasn't going to let a thing like body weakness get in the way of escaping. Figuring out how to get back to Logan gave me some strength.

The last time I'd gone to him had been during a storm, and I'd climbed the hill toward his castle. When lightning struck, I'd been transported. But I knew from Moira and

Shona's story, they'd both traveled back in time from their house in Edinburgh. It didn't seem to matter where you were, as long as the circumstances were right and Fate decided it was time.

All I had to do was get to Edinburgh. To...what street did they live on? I couldn't remember the name of it, but I knew where they kept a spare key. And I knew that everyone knew them. Someone could point me in the right direction.

I glanced toward the ground, ten feet from where I was and nothing to shimmy down on. This wasn't going to feel good.

I could break a leg, twist an ankle.

But it would be worth it. I'd crawl all the way to Edinburgh if I had to, just to get away from Steven.

I took a deep breath and closed my eyes. The air was wet, and I could smell Loch Ness not far in the distance. Twisting so that I faced the inside of the tiny room, I had one leg hanging free and the other hooked over the ledge.

Somehow, I managed to tug the other leg out, hanging on for dear life with quivering arms. I lowered myself, clutching to the windowsill with fingers that were slowly slipping. Face to face with white clapboard, mold growing along its edges. Only about a five foot drop now. Not too far.

One. Two. Three.

I closed my eyes. Braced myself. And let go.

My toes hit quickly, a painful jarring up my legs.

I ignored the fact that I was dressed in the clothes of the sixteenth century and barefoot.

"Mrs. Gordon..." I whirled to see Mrs. Lamb poking her head out of the back door. "Here. Take it, please."

She held out a beige, leather pocketbook. Without thinking, I grabbed the purse and gave Mrs. Lamb a tight hug.

"Go," she urged.

I heard a commotion, something slamming above, fanning down from the opened window I'd jumped out.

"Go, now!" Mrs. Lamb pushed me and I ran through her yard, tripping on an uprooted tree root, catching myself at the last second.

"Emma!" Steven's bellow cut through the air, louder than a canon. "Get back here, you bitch!"

But I didn't stop running. Didn't turn around to look at him. Didn't want to see the angry, twisting snarl on his face. Afraid that if I did, I'd trip and fall and he'd catch up to me.

I shoved open the gate at the back of Mrs. Lamb's yard, rushing through several yards before making it to a street. I ran all the way down the road, around the corner, my feet slapping painfully against the sidewalk, bits of acorn and other debris digging into the soles of my feet.

"Mrs. Gordon!" An older woman pushed open the door of her tiny yellow house and waved at me. "Mrs. Lamb called. Come in!"

I didn't even ask. I bolted inside, let her shut the door behind me and set the lock in place.

I leaned against the wall beside the door, panting, my head hitting and rocking a picture that hung there.

"Thank you," I murmured, pressing my hand to my heart.

The woman nodded, her lips pursed. "Never ye mind that, dear. We need to get ye cleaned up."

"I'm—"

"Emma." She gripped my hand in hers, patted it. "I know, dearie. I'm Mrs. MacDonald. We've all been hearing about ye. Come now. I've a daughter about your size. We'll get ye changed and then I'll drive ye wherever ye need."

I let myself breathe a small, hopeful, sigh of relief. "Edinburgh. I need to get to Edinburgh."

"I'll take ye there."

"But it's so far from here." At least a four-hour drive. "Maybe just the train station."

"Nonsense. No distance is too far." She sounded like she wanted to add more, perhaps that she'd drive to Hell if needed to get me away from Steven.

We've all been hearing about ye.

Thank God for Mrs. Lamb. She was like my fairy grandmother in this world. I hadn't the inclination to be annoyed that she'd been talking about me, for I was only grateful that she had, or else I'd not be here, dry and almost safe.

Mrs. MacDonald ushered me up a narrow staircase, the fact that her name was the same as Logan's greatest enemy not lost on me.

She led me into a small bedroom, wallpapered in thistles, and looking as though it had been last decorated in 1968. A yellowed, crocheted blanket covered a twin bed pushed up against the wall. A tall, antique dresser stood stoically beside the window, with a basin and pitcher on top.

She flung open a closet, and the clothes inside also looked like they were from 1968. The woman looked to be in her seventies, making her daughter maybe in her forties or fifties at most.

"Claudia likes vintage, as ye can tell," Mrs. MacDonald frowned, riffling through the clothes. "'Haps this will do."

She tugged out a plain black, knee-length, cotton wrap dress. A thick black belt to tie in the middle. Two black, leather flats.

I worked to shuck myself from the wet linen and wool, the fabric sticking to my skin. But finally, I stood naked, arms crossed over my full breasts, dripping and achy.

Mrs. MacDonald looked me over, appraising me with a sorrowful eye.

"A bath first?"

"Is there time?" I glanced toward the window where the blinds were drawn.

"He's not going to look for ye so close. And even if he comes knocking, I don't have to answer."

I nodded, a small weight lifting, and feeling grateful to have people on my side.

"Come along then." She handed me a bathrobe, which I slipped on, the feel of the scratchy old terrycloth a reminder of the one my mother used to wear before she died.

"When did ye have your bairn?" she asked.

I swallowed hard, again touching the softness of my belly. "Saor was born six weeks ago."

"Saor. I like that name. Seems fitting, given your situation." She cocked her head, like she was going to say more but instead, said, "We'll get ye back to Saor."

I nodded, even though I was pretty certain Mrs. MacDonald had no idea how to get me back to my child. Or that I'd even time traveled in the first place.

❧ 2 ❧

LOGAN

July, 1544

I woke with a start, the bed beside me cold. Saor wailed in his cradle, the same one I'd howled in as a bairn. Carved oak, a tale of our history etched in the posts, much the same as the four-poster I shared with my wife.

"Emma?" I sat up in the bed, swinging off the covers, standing nude.

I turned in a circle, stretching and frowning. Our chamber was empty save for Saor and I. His tiny fists of fury punched at the sky as he yowled at the injustice of having been left alone.

"Where is your mama?" I crooned to the tiny lad, lifting him from his cradle and sticking my finger in his gummy mouth to suck on until she came back. "Must have gone to the privy."

Of course, there had to be a logical reason behind Emma leaving our chamber, and the privy it must have been. My mind wanted to travel toward another explanation, however, as it often did if I couldn't find her right away. One we'd both feared would come. If she'd been brought to me from another time, when would she be taken away?

I refused to think of that. But it was odd that she was missing, given she normally used the chamber pot in the middle of the night. But, mayhap, her stomach was feeling unwell and she needed privacy.

I paced the room with the bairn sucking at my finger until that no longer satisfied and his wails once more climbed up to echo in the rafters.

Many minutes had passed and with each ensuing second, I became more and more worried about what could have happened to my wife.

Granted our child was only six weeks old, but in the past several weeks, she'd not once left in the middle of the night. Nor had she done so the entirety of the time she carried the child within her womb.

Unable to wait another moment, I placed the bairn back in his cradle, his cries growing louder as I tugged on breeches, not bothering to tie them closed. I scooped Saor back up, wrapping him in a soft plaid blanket and opened the door, carrying him out to the corridor. The bairn quieted, his tiny eyes roving over the change in place. All was quiet; the moon still high in the sky and darkness blanketed the Highlands.

"Emma?" I called, walking down the length of the long corridor toward the end, my feet silent on the stone floor. The doorway to the privy chamber was slightly ajar, no light from a candle seeping through the opening.

The closer I got, the quieter the night seemed to become. The stiller the air, as though we were the only two beings in the world.

"Emma?" I called again, and still she did not answer.

I pushed open the door, finding the privy empty, the stench of waste made worse by the heat of the summer.

Saor whimpered, shoving his fists against his tiny lips.

I frowned, asking the bairn, again, "Where is your mama?"

In answer, Saor howled, his little body growing tense with his anger, his back arching.

"My laird?"

A sleepy looking nursemaid opened the door to the chamber she'd been housed in across the hall from Emma's and mine, in case she was ever needed, though Emma had yet to call on the lass.

"Can ye take the bairn? Have ye seen Lady Emma?"

The woman rubbed at her eyes and shook her head. "I'll take him, and nay, my laird, I haven't."

I handed the bairn over to the tired lass; ignoring the appreciative glance she gave my bare chest. It never ceased to fail, a fact I used to be proud of but now found exceedingly irritating.

"Keep him until morn." If—*nay, when*—I found Emma, I was going to lay her out across the bed and make sweet, raw, love to her.

Mayhap Emma had gone to the kitchens, hungry. She'd barely eaten any of her supper; too tired was she with caring for the bairn all by herself. I helped where I could, but I'd yet to grow breasts. That thought made me chuckle. I normally insisted she remain in our chamber to rest throughout the day, but I was certain she snuck around the castle while I was out with the men. Emma loved to be involved with the day-to-day things, and I admired her for it. But often, she let herself suffer rather than take the rest she deserved.

With long, hurried strides, I made my way back down the corridor toward the stairs, taking them three at a time until I reached the bottom. The guards there leapt to alertness.

"All is well, my laird," one of them grumbled, wiping at his sleepy eyes.

"What of my wife? Have ye seen Lady Emma?"

"Not since yestermorn, my laird," the second guard said, much more alert than the first.

Yestermorn. So, she'd not come down the stairs. I regarded the men, puzzled. "'Haps ye fell asleep and missed her."

"Nay, my laird," the alert guard responded. "I've been awake the whole time."

"As have I, my laird." The second guard looked slightly worried that I wouldn't believe him. "She's not come this way. Shall we help ye to find her?"

I frowned. She could have gone down the servant's stair, but why would she do an odd thing like that?

"Nay. Man your posts and if ye do see her, please ask her to wait for me in our chamber, and one of ye come to find me."

The guards nodded their agreement.

I made my way toward the kitchens, finding it empty save for the sleeping form of a couple kitchen boys by the hearth. In an hour or so, Cook would wake and begin the days' baking, and the lads would rise to help her.

I cleared my throat, approaching the lads who leapt to their feet, swiping hands over their grimy faces, rubbing crust from their eyes.

"Have ye seen Lady Emma?" I asked them, though I doubted either of them would have woken had she come inside, since they'd not even stirred when I entered the kitchens.

"Nay, my laird," they both said in unison.

"Ballocks!" Where the hell was she? I scraped a hand through my hair, that one fear, that she'd disappeared niggling at the base of my skull, a fingernail scratching at an open wound.

Rory had disappeared from the Highlands for five long years. Shona had gone back to the present to find Moira. They'd all returned. But that didn't mean that Emma would, and even if she did, it might be years. I shook my head. *Nay, nay, nay.* She was here. I just hadn't found her yet.

I circled back to the servants' stair, checking with the guard posted there who also hadn't seen her, either. If none of the guards posted at the stairs had seen her come down, then 'haps she'd gone up?

She liked to take walks on the battlements often, breathing in the fresh air, taking a few private moments to think.

I took the stairs three at a time, once more, all the way to the top, but the door to the battlements was bolted. Was it possible she'd gone out and someone bolted it behind her?

Doubtful, but possible.

I unlocked the door and pushed it open, feeling the coolness of the summer night wash over my skin. This side of the castle was empty of guards at this time of night. Several others were stationed at key points, but since Emma liked it up here, and I sometimes joined her for privacy, this particular turret was often unmanned.

And it was empty now.

"Emma?" I called anyway, hoping she'd poke her head from some crevice I couldn't see her behind.

Guards on the other walls turned toward me, and I raised my arm in greeting. I'd have to question each one of them. Someone must have seen something.

I made my way around the unoccupied turret. Panic, which had started the moment I found her side of the bed empty, curled deep in my gut, shredding me from the inside out.

She was gone.

People often disappeared in the Highlands, but there was only one reason for a person to vanish into thin air and I didn't want to think about what that meant.

Fate *could not* have recalled her.

I refused to believe it. Refused to allow such a horrifying notion to even take root—but it already had. For, when I'd found out about Emma, wasn't this the one thing I'd feared the most?

I approached each guard on the battlements, every guard at the front gates, the postern gate, and the water gate... None had seen her. Murmurings of the castle walls being breached by the enemy sent up a panic. And it wasn't like I could quell that panic or naysay their assumptions. They didn't know about time travel, or about Emma's past. To them, their mistress had been taken, secreted away from the castle by some nefarious criminal.

"What's going on?" Ewan approached from the castle, looking harried. The sun was starting to rise, but the shadows on his features were all concern.

I gritted my teeth and then finally put my voice to work, hearing the way I sounded choked when I spoke. "I canna find Emma."

Ewan's face paled, visible in the dim dawn light. The way his eyes shuttered, I knew he had the same fear as I. Emma was his sister. If she could disappear, it meant he could—or his wife. Hell. Ewan wasn't even from this time. He'd traveled years ago and never returned—save for a twenty-four hour period.

"When was the last time ye saw her?" Ewan asked.

"When she was feeding Saor in our chamber, afore bed." The two of them had been so beautiful. Her fiery red curls, their sons matching locks. She'd cradled him to her breast, smiling down at the bairn as though he were an angel beckoning her. They were both my angels.

Ewan frowned. "Do ye think...?"

He trailed off, but I knew what he was thinking. The same thing as I. Neither one of us wanted to say it out loud for fear it would be true. Giving voice to thoughts often made them more powerful.

I shook my head. "Nay, it canna be." I ground my teeth so hard I feared they'd turn to dust, pain pounded through my skull. "Fate canna do this to me."

I felt as though someone had shoved a jagged-edged dirk into my chest and was sawing back and forth very slowly at my heart.

"Fate can do whatever she wishes," Ewan muttered. He raked a hand through his hair and blew out a breath. He and Emma had been separated when they were both children, a plane crash that she'd thought had claimed her brother's life, but in fact sent him here to me as a lad. They'd only just found out about each other.

Fate can do whatever she wishes. Damn Fate to hell!

That was not what I wanted to hear, that all power and control over the situation had been stripped from me. I liked being in control, needed it, and craved it.

"I will scour the earth for her before I believe that she's been taken," I said.

Ewan let out a long, downtrodden sigh. "Do ye remember doing the same thing when I went missing a few months ago?"

I gave a brief, curt nod, pulling my lips back from my teeth and hissing. Nay, nay, nay. She *needed* to be here. *I need her. I love her.*

Ewan regarded me with steady, serious eyes. "It didna help."

"Ye're not helping," I growled.

Ewan nodded. "Haps not. I will go and check with the guards."

"I've already done it."

"I'll check with those who are asleep then."

I could tell he was only going through the motions. Ewan had already determined that Emma had time traveled.

"Aye. Wake them all. We will check the surroundings of the castle in case one of my enemies has somehow managed to breach the walls."

Ewan pressed his lips together, obviously wanting to say more, but he didn't. He jogged off to do my bidding, and though we had somewhat of a plan in place, I didn't feel better, not even a twinge. I felt worse. For, I was beginning to believe that she was truly gone.

How could I get her back?

Mayhap Shona, the Lady of the Wood as she'd been dubbed years before, would know what to do. Married to Ewan, she lived here at the castle now, the castle healer, and she was due to have her own bairn in a month's time.

If she didn't know how, mayhap Emma had told her something, anything, that might help me to find her. Emma had been the one who often listened the most to local folklore or the minstrel's tales as they were sung, asking questions and investigating. It had been her idea to make love by the sacred stone in order to conceive our child. The magic of the stone had worked.

What else might she know? How could I find her?

"Emma!" I bellowed toward the sky, disturbing the crows that'd come to perch on the walls, awaiting the movement of anything they might find appetizing.

"My laird." Shona's soft fingers slid over my elbow.

"Where is she? Did she tell ye she was leaving me?" I asked, almost desperate for that to be the answer so at least I knew she was alive and here somewhere that I could find her and beg her to take me back.

Shona's hands lifted to her massive pregnant belly and she shook her head. "She did not mention leaving. I think..." She frowned, her lips pursing. "I think she has, ye know... Left..."

"How could ye think that?"

"I had a dream."

"A vision?"

Shona shook her head. "I dinna get visions. 'Twas a dream."

"Tell me."

"I dreamt that Emma was running down a street, but it was a modern street. Rain was falling and she was looking behind her, alarm in her eyes."

"Was someone chasing her?"

"Nay, not that I could see. But it was so real." She stroked her belly, and I could see a wave of movement as the bairn inside her did a somersault. "I've never had a dream so vivid. I felt like if I just reached my arms out long enough, I could grab hold of her."

"I need to find her. I need to go to her."

Shona glanced toward the ground. "When we, the four of us, came back..." She was referring to the time that her, Ewan, Moira and Rory returned to the Highlands from their modern world. But Shona didn't continue.

"What?"

She looked me in the eyes and I saw sorrow there, guilt. "We wondered if by coming back it would force someone to leave."

"Why would ye think that?"

Shona shrugged. "I dinna know much about time travel. Why, how or even what, but I do know that nature has a balance of things, and she works hard to keep that balance."

I ground my teeth, not wanting to put to voice the dark

thoughts going through my mind. Emma had been a blessing brought to me a couple years before. Without her, I'd still be locked in the deep dark of my mind. But she'd brought with her a light. Something good I could grasp onto, and I'd felt her pull, felt her haul me out of that darkness.

"I want her back."

"I know."

"Help me."

"I can try." But she looked doubtful. "Perhaps a trip to the grove? To the stone circle?"

I scrubbed a hand over my face, feeling bereft and determined at the same time.

Ewan returned to me then, a slight shake of his head. "No one has seen her."

"Scour the woods, the roads, the village," I ordered. "I'm going to the sacred grove."

Ewan nodded. "I'll see it done, my laird."

"Did ye dream, Logan?" Shona asked.

I shook my head. "Not this time..." My voice trailed off as I recalled those odd dreams from years before.

When I'd been captured and strapped to a table in the torturer's chamber, Emma had come to me in a dream. She'd given me strength and I'd been able to escape.

Now, Shona had a dream of Emma in another time. Mayhap the way to get her back was through dreams.

I marched toward the water gate. "Open the gates," I demanded.

I yanked a boat from where it was moored, and seized the oars. Prepared to make my way across the loch.

❦ 3 ❦

EMMA

Present Day

Less than four hours after climbing into Mrs. MacDonald's compact, blue Vauxhall, we pulled off the A90 onto Belford Road. We'd found Shona and Moira's address in an old tattered phonebook—and I was exceedingly grateful, and surprised, that it wasn't unlisted.

I grabbed for the *oh shit* handle near the top of the passenger side window—again, my other hand clutched the beige, fabric seat.

The woman drove like a maniac.

Not at all what one would expect from someone in her aged years. My hands ached from holding tight the entirety of the ride. I was a little dizzy from being whipped around.

The countryside had sped past us in beautiful blurs of green, orange, red and yellow. If I squinted my eyes enough to blur out the modern corners of the houses and shops we passed, it could almost pass for 1544.

Mrs. MacDonald whipped the car around to the right, nearly taking out a mother pushing a stroller—which sent my heart into palpitations of sorrow and fear.

Oh, Saor. How was my baby?

The mother shouted, shaking her fist at us, but Mrs. MacDonald barely seemed to notice. My gut ached from her neglect for their safety.

I was honestly surprised we'd made it here alive. The car jerked to a stop, and I slapped my hand on the dash to keep from hitting my head. We'd finally reached Coates Garden where Moira and Shona had lived.

"That's it there, lass." She pulled up in front of a pretty, stone, row home. Flowers in the window-baskets wilted over the side, dead.

Trees lining the street had lost most of their leaves, but a few orange and red ones hung on for dear life. Lampposts dotted the sidewalk, and I imagined then when it grew dark, this was a picturesque street.

A woman a few houses down from the Ayreshires swept her broom with fury on the path, eyeing us with curiosity. From Shona's description of her matronly, nosy neighbor, I recognized her instantly. Stout and big bosomed. Her graying hair was pulled back in a bun that frayed at the sides. It had probably been neater that morning, but fallen loose from the head whipping she must do as she snooped on her neighbors.

What had Shona said her neighbor's name was?

I couldn't remember, and quite frankly, I didn't care. I wasn't going to make friends, let alone speak to her. The less people knew who I was, the better.

"Is this your place?" Mrs. MacDonald asked again, even though she'd asked me the same thing when she looked in the phonebook.

I could tell she wanted to know more. Wanted to ask me a thousand questions. But I didn't have any answers for her.

The effort to talk seemed like too much. I couldn't tell her the whole truth, and then I'd have to try and remember what I'd omitted and what I'd made up. I'd just need to stick to simple facts. Mundane truths. Kind of like what I had to do when I'd first met Logan, so he wouldn't know at the time that I was from another time. I was amazed and grateful that he'd listened to my truth when I was ready, and accepted it. Loving me no matter what.

"No." I shook my head and reached for the car handle, wanting to escape the small car and breathe in deeply of the cool November air. I felt like I was suffocating under her prying gaze and the secrets I kept. "My friends' house." I glanced at Mrs. MacDonald, saw that she'd turned the key in the ignition and was making way to climb out of the vehicle. "Thanks for dropping me off," I said, hoping, but not hopeful, that she would take the hint I didn't want her to come inside.

It was uncharitable of me. After four hours in the car, her old bladder most likely needed to relieve itself, I knew I did, and she might want a cup of tea, or even to stay for a while before making her way back. I couldn't blame her. That was a lot of driving, and I'd not want to whip around and return, even if I knew Steven wasn't there.

"I'm coming in." Her words were filled with conviction, and so I didn't argue.

After all, the woman had saved me from Steven. A virtual stranger. I owed her more than she even realized.

"All right," I said wearily, climbing from the car.

I made my way up the short walk to the front door, surreptitiously glancing down the street.

The nosy neighbor waddled faster than Mrs. MacDonald drove, up the walk toward us. I recalled what Shona told me about this woman. How she stuck her nose into everyone's business—as though it were her life's purpose to know everything about everyone. How they'd been terrified that she would figure out what they were up to when they'd come home from jail still in cellblock uniform. How they'd lied and said they were in their workout clothes.

"Excuse me," she said. "Have you seen the Ayreshire lassies?"

I forced a smile on my face and rounded to meet her meddlesome regard. "Why, yes, I have." My voice sounded entirely too cheerful and fake to my own ears.

"Oh." She squinted her eyes, looking me up and down and then doing the same to Mrs. MacDonald. Thank God I couldn't hear her thoughts. "Where are they?"

So blunt, she was. I guess I didn't expect anything different.

"They went on a vacation," I said, the first thing that came to mind.

"A vacation." She narrowed her eyes, and I kept my gaze steady, going for the look a teacher gave a student when questioned. "For several weeks."

She wasn't asking, but stating a fact, and it came out rather judgmentally.

I nodded, not feeling required to explain their situation to an outsider.

"We're here to take care of the house," Mrs. MacDonald added.

I glanced back at her, wondering why she felt the need to step in.

Did the old broad know something about time traveling? *Ohmygod...*

I had to be reading into things. Paranoid about everything and everyone. She was probably just coming to my rescue from the pesky busybody. Wanted to escape this conversation as much as I did.

The neighbor sniffed, swiping hair from her face. "Well, ye'll need the key then."

I turned to face her, narrowing my eyes and cocking my head. I refrained from putting my hands on my hips, reasoning this would likely only get the lady riled up more. "Did you take their key?"

She straightened, holding her broom firm and straight up and down on the ground, like a Roman sentry with his spear. "I did."

I cocked my head, genuinely irritated and curious. "Why would you do that?"

Her nose turned up. "I wasn't certain they'd be back." Her eyes shifted away.

"That's an odd thing to say. They are your neighbors, and have been so for quite some time. There is no for sale sign. Why would you think that?"

She pursed her lips and looked me straight in the eye. "On account of them having broken out of jail."

I couldn't help but laugh. "Jail?"

Mrs. MacDonald eyed me with worry, but I shook my head. So she'd not fallen for their lie about working as personal trainers. She was smarter than they thought. Or just more of a busybody than anyone had anticipated. Probably went home and searched on the internet for what the clothes at the jail looked like.

She smacked the broom against the pavement. "Jail, missy."

"You've got the wrong of it," I said, using the tone I carried with wayward staff or adolescents at Gealach Castle. "And it is unchristian of you to pass judgments, especially false. I hope you haven't spread rumors like this across town. I'd hate for Shona and Moira to return from the U.S. and be labeled for something they didn't do."

"Well, I..." The woman sputtered.

"Best give us back the key, else I'll be forced to call the police," Mrs. MacDonald said. "That's stealing, and at your age, ye ought to know better. I'm certain ye don't want to spend a night in jail."

I had to bite the inside of my cheek to keep from laughing. The neighbor was likely every bit the same age as Mrs. MacDonald. But the mention of stealing, and spending the night in jail, seemed to drain her of her attitude.

"I'll go get it," she muttered, but then waggled her finger at me. "But I've got my eye on ye. Any funny business and I'll see to it that the police are questioning *ye*."

I was too tired to respond, and when Mrs. MacDonald said she would follow the neighbor back to her house to retrieve the key I nodded, sitting down on the front stoop, all the energy sapped from me. I pressed my forehead to my palms, massaged my temples, the pounding in my head not having abated.

"Where are you, Logan?" I murmured into my hands.

But there was no answer, as I knew there wouldn't be. Oh, but I could have curled up on the stoop and cried. My entire body ached for missing my family. Tears pricked my eyes and I blinked them away, not wanting to break down in front of my new friend. I'd already burdened her enough.

A moment later, Mrs. MacDonald returned with a bronze colored key and held it out to me.

"I don't know what that was about, my dear, but we'd best get inside before the old biddy comes at ye again. I can tell ye're tired."

I nodded, took the key and forced myself to stand. With great effort, as my limbs felt heavy, thick, tired, I slipped the key into the lock. The bolt turned easier than any at Gealach, and I pushed the door open.

The inside of the house was dark and smelled slightly of stale air. The blinds were drawn. I expected, with them having been gone, to also smell something rotten, since they'd not had a chance to empty their trash or clean out the fridge before Fate pulled them back to 1544. I was surprised to find I didn't.

I flipped a switch and lights turned on. The neighbor said they'd been gone a few weeks, so the electric company wouldn't have turned off their power just yet. Thank goodness, for me.

"Can I get you some tea?" I asked, walking down the corridor toward the back of the house, where a kitchen normally is, and pleased to see I found it.

I didn't want Mrs. MacDonald to realize I'd never been here before. I was also hoping she said no.

"How about ye sit down and I'll make the tea." Mrs. MacDonald scooted past me, patting my shoulder as she went.

I nodded, slumping into a wooden kitchen table chair and settling the pocket book Mrs. Lamb gave me onto the tabletop. I'd yet to look inside, but guessed there was money. Why else would she insist I take it?

I should have offered to give Mrs. MacDonald money for gas. She'd volunteered the eight hour round trip, but she shouldn't have to pay for it. I opened the purse to find a wallet with several hundred pound bills in it.

Ohmygod...

If there was such a thing as a fairy godmother—which I wouldn't be surprised to find out given there was such a thing as time travel—then Mrs. Lamb was she.

"Let me give you money for gas," I said.

"No need, dearie." Mrs. MacDonald was busy heating up water in the electric kettle, and sticking tea bags into two black coffee cups.

"Please, let me." I tugged out a bill and held it out to her.

"Nay, dear. I couldn't. It wouldn't be right." She opened and closed a few drawers, finding a spoon, and then cleared her throat. "There is fresh cream in the refrigerator."

"Oh?"

"Aye. Someone has been here recently."

I nodded. "Likely my friends." I had no way of knowing whether or not they'd been gone as long as their neighbor accused. She could be senile. Sometimes years passed when a person time traveled, other times minutes. "I'll check the expiration date."

"Already did. Doesn't expire for another week."

"Oh, good." My voice trailed off. All I could think about was Logan and Saor. Nothing as stupid as cream for my tea.

"Where is your son?"

It was as if she'd read my thoughts. I bit my lip. Was I so obvious? I leaned back further in the chair, praying I could just sink into the wood and end up back in 1544. "He is with his father," I managed to answer.

"That man?" She winged a brow, her frown deepening her wrinkles. "Steven?"

I shook my head. "No. Not him."

"Ah." She didn't ask any more questions. That one sound seeming to bring her to her own conclusions and I let her think whatever it was she wanted. What did I care what she thought about me, or whether or not her judgments would ruin a reputation that I cared nothing for? I didn't belong here. I wasn't going to stay. Her conclusions, and anyone else's, mattered little to me.

As we sipped our tea in silence, an opened bag of short-bread cookies on the table, two missing from Mrs. MacDonald, none from me, the sun started to set, shrouding the kitchen in shadows.

My limbs buzzed with nerves and I realized I didn't want to be alone. Not tonight.

Mrs. MacDonald stood up to turn on a dim light over the table.

"Mrs. MacDonald..." I set my teacup down. "Do you want

to stay the night? I'd hate for you to drive all the way back to Drumnadrochit in the dark."

Her smile was filled with relief. "Oh, thank ye. That would be nice."

I glanced up at the ceiling, not sure what the bedroom situation was. There had to be at least two with both sisters having lived here.

"I'll fix ye some supper. Ye look as though ye could use a hot meal."

I nodded. "Do you mind if I go and lay down? I'm so tired."

"Go on. I'll wake ye when it's time to eat."

I stood up from the table, and walked heavily toward the stairs, exhaustion leaping from my limbs. I grabbed the railing, and it felt like I used more of my upper body to hoist myself up the stairs than my legs.

Upstairs, I found three bedrooms. Each one with beds made. Two were clearly the bedrooms of Moira and Shona, and the third was a guest room. I figured Mrs. MacDonald could take the guest room and I'd take Shona's room. According to their story, Shona hadn't been home for years, but her bedroom looked like she'd just left that morning. Not a spec of dust.

On the nightstand was a book, *The Highlander's Reward*, with a bookmark near the end. She'd never gotten the chance to finish it. That was sad. I'd heard a few ladies at the grocery store once talking about it. How they loved it. Steven didn't allow romance novels in the house, so I'd never had the chance. I'd have to take it with me. I slipped it into the pocketbook, knowing Shona would be excited to get it back.

I flipped the light out and lay down on the bed, flopping my arm over my eyes, not bothering with the covers. Within seconds I was drifting, floating, my body sinking into an exhausted sleep.

"Emma..." The sound of Logan's voice was far off. A soft sound that drew me into the darkness. "Emma..."

I let myself fall into sleep, dreaming of my husband. My love.

I was in a grove. The one up on the mountain, with the sacred stone. Logan stood in the center, his arm outstretched, beckoning me forward. His dark hair, loose around his shoulders, blew gently in the breeze, eyes as intense as I remembered. He was shirtless, a pair of breeches, untied, hung from his hips. His body was everything I remembered, strength and power and sexuality melted into one stunning figure.

"Ye came," he said, his voice gravelly and deep.

"I miss you," I said, rushing forward, feeling as though I were floating. All the heaviness, the exhaustion I'd felt, was gone, replaced with a feeling of elation. I was thankful that sleep could bring me to him. Was it a dream? Or was it like before... Where our spirits had met in the middle? If I was wondering, didn't that mean that it was the latter? For if it were truly a dream, would I be asking myself those questions?

"Where did ye go?" he asked, wrapping me up in his tall, strong embrace. His skin was warm, corded muscle taut beneath. "Are ye safe?"

"I am here with you," I said. "And safe as I can be at the moment." I couldn't tell him about Steven just yet, and have him worry.

"Nay, ye are not really. Where are ye?"

I swallowed and reached up to touch his face, to stare into his dark eyes. So, I was right. This was our spirits meeting. "I am at Shona and Moira's house in Edinburgh."

"In modern day?"

"Yes," I whispered.

His eyes turned stormy and I could see he wrestled with the same despair coursing through my veins. "How? How can this be?"

I shook my head, pressing my hands flat and firm onto his back, tears wetting his hot skin.

"I don't know. I remember falling asleep in your arms, and then when I woke—" My voice lurched, and I choked on a sob. I couldn't speak anymore.

Logan swiped at the tears tracking down my cheeks. "My love," he murmured in Gaelic. "Do not cry. Ye must be strong. I am here."

I shook my head again. "No, you're not. You're just a dream."

"I am here. 'Tis me. Kiss me and ye'll see."

I looked up into his dark eyes, filled with mysteries I'd solved and some I'd yet to uncover. I wanted to melt with him. To forget where I was and what had happened. I leaned up on tiptoe and touched my lips to his. They were warm, firm yet soft, and familiar. But no matter how familiar, whenever I kissed him, my body sparked. Tingles shot through my limbs.

We'd not made love since before Saor was born, and even though this was a dream, I tucked my body close to his, wanting to feel him touch me, to sink inside me.

Logan's tongue traced the outline of my lips before delving inside to tangle with mine. He tasted sweet and spicy and utterly intoxicating. He cupped my cheek with one hand and wrapped his other arm around my waist.

"*Mo chreach*, it's been so long," he murmured against my lips.

Beneath my bare feet, the soft grass of the grove cushioned me. The stone behind him glowed and the air was charged with a heat and energy that sank deep into my bones.

"This feels so real," I murmured.

"'Tis."

I shook my head, not wanting to ruin the mood by telling my dream husband that he wasn't real.

"Remember when MacDonald took me? Remember when ye came to me in a dream and made love to me?"

My eyes widened, for I'd thought the same thing before, and nearly dismissed it as wishful thinking. "Yes."

"I am here to give ye strength, my love, to find me again. Fate has made a mistake."

❧ 4 ❧

LOGAN

"We shouldn't have been separated. Whatever the mistake was, we'll correct it." I flashed a confident grin, watched her search my eyes, and then she returned my smile.

"Ever the strong warrior, husband. With you, I feel like we could take on the world and win." Her arms tightened around me, warm, her gaze filled with trust.

"The world, the Fates." I shrugged and chuckled, nuzzling her hair behind her ear and breathing in her scent. "I'm going to make love to ye, Emma. Here. Now."

I skimmed my lips over her cheek, pressing my forehead to hers, locking eyes. Color brushed her cheeks, an impish smile on her lips.

I gazed down at my wife, perfectly ethereal and yet flesh, blood and silky locks, standing before me. All voluptuous curves and sensuality.

"Take off your clothes," I murmured.

Emma took a step away from me, her red wavy hair glossy in the light of sunset. Her blue eyes fastened on mine, full of confidence, love, lust, as she tugged the tie at the waist of the odd black gown she wore.

"Ye're beautiful," I said, feeling my throat tighten. I'd always thought her stunning, but now that she was gone from me...

It was hard to think. Hard to breathe.

The gown unraveled around her body, much like my mind, unwinding to a pool of mush. Normally, I was the one in control. But today...

Now...

I knew what was at stake.

Her.

The beautiful life we'd built together.

Beneath the gown she wore undergarments much like what she'd had on the day we'd first met. White with lace trim. Her belly was slightly round from her pregnancy, soft, and I reached out to circle my finger around her belly button.

She pressed a hand over my fingers, stilling me.

"Don't," she said, embarrassment flashing on her face, before she ducked her chin toward her chest.

"Why?" I touched a finger to her chin, urging her to look at me.

She glanced down, a flicker of emotion that I recognized crossing her features. I'd not seen her look like that in a long time. Self-conscious. Emma started to tug the gown closed again, but I stopped her, pushing the fabric off her shoulders.

"I am... not the same," she answered.

"Och, but ye're right." I slid the fabric over her arms, all the way to her wrists exposing her back, her chest. "Ye're exquisite." I dropped to my knees in front of her and pressed my lips to her belly, placed a hand on either side of her navel. "And this is where ye carried our child. I'm proud of ye. More than ye could ever imagine, and I'd never shun ye for birthing our bairn, for how your body changed from carrying him. Please, dinna shame yourself."

Tears sparked her eyes and she touched my cheek. "How did I get so lucky?"

"'Tis I who am lucky, lass. Being with ye has forever changed me for the better. 'Tis like having the sun and moon and stars all nestled beside me."

"I love you so much," she said, her words hurried and filled with emotion. Her hands threaded through my hair, tugging, as she liked to do.

"I love ye so verra much, too." I wrapped my arms around her hips, pressed my face to her belly, breathing in her herbal and floral scent. Familiar, comforting. Tears stung my eyes. I squeezed them shut, not wanting Emma to see me cry. I was a man. Men didn't cry, and yet I was so overcome with emotion, distress. Need. Love.

We might have both been asleep right now, dreaming of each other five hundred years apart, but we were still together, and when she woke, I didn't want her to think that I was a blubbering fool.

I needed to lose myself in her flesh. To enjoy what little time Fate had given us as a reprieve. I massaged the backs of her legs, up to her round arse, cupping the cheeks as I rubbed my lips back and forth over the skin just below her belly button, breathing hotly until she whimpered and gooseflesh rose beneath my fingertips.

I didn't want her to leave, but I didn't know how long we had either. We could both be awakened at any moment, the spell broken. Would Fate give us another chance to dream of one another? Would making love one time be enough to bring me to her or transport her back to me?

Emma got down on her knees in front of me, cupping my face with her long, delicate hands. She kissed me deeply, wiping away wetness that appeared on my cheeks, and I realized my tears had fallen, and she'd caught me crying.

But she didn't say anything, just kissed me in that way she had that sucked the breath from me, and yet, made me feel as though I were wrapped up in warmth.

I was the warrior. I was the Guardian of Scotland. I was Laird Grant, and yet, the touch of my wife, her love, could cut me at the knees like nothing else.

Emma gently pushed at my shoulders until I lay on my back with her climbing over me. She stroked her long fingers over my shoulders, my chest, tracing a path over every muscle until she skated over my abdomen toward my rock-hard cock. She untied my breeches the rest of the way and set my solid length free.

Och, how I ached for her. Blood surged toward my middle, filling my shaft until it was thicker, longer than it had been in years.

I supposed my dreams would give me a bit more than my already well-endowed cock possessed.

"Oh," Emma gasped as she reached my length, wrapping her fingers around my hot skin and then sliding upward.

"All for ye, lass." I flashed a wicked grin, and winked.

She smiled down at me. "Every inch."

I leaned up and worked to remove the odd bits of lace from her breasts, trying to free them. Wanting to touch. To lick. They were larger than before. She gently pushed my hands away and covered herself.

"Not this time...," her voice trailed off, that self-consciousness rearing its head again.

I nodded, wanting to comply with her wishes, not wanting to ruin anything by pushing her in a way she wasn't comfortable with. She started to tuck the garment back on, when a thought occurred to me. I realized why she might not want me to touch her breasts, as she used them to feed our son; perhaps she was self-conscious of that fact.

"Ye know this is a dream," I said. "There will be no milk... spillage."

Her face lit up, her mouth forming a surprised O. "Oh, I didn't think of that. In that case..." She tugged off the lace, and I moved in quick to cup the fleshy globes, rubbing my lips over one pert nipple and my thumb over the other.

Emma groaned, her head falling back, a pink flush covering her silky skin. "That feels so good."

"Better than good," I replied, flicking my tongue over her softness.

She tasted of peaches, honey and everything I ever wanted.

Emma straddled my hips, her sex pressed hotly to my cock. Through the silky undergarment I could feel how wet she was, and it made my blood burn with the need to feel her hot flesh naked on mine.

"I'm going to rip these off," I said, taking hold of the garment and shredding them with one tug. "I need to be inside ye."

Emma giggled. "I hope I don't wake up naked."

"I hope ye do," I growled, sliding my fingers between her silken folds and shuddering at the contact. I gently pinched the throbbing nub, she called it her clit, and she cried out. "Damn, lass, ye're so wet."

Emma dropped her lips to my shoulder, nipping my skin and then licking and sucking every place she put her teeth.

"Get inside me, Logan," she demanded.

The roles were quickly reversed, with my wife taking charge and ordering me about. But I didn't mind. It had been months since I'd felt the silken heat of her flesh wrapped around my cock.

I gripped the base of my erection and slid it along her wet

folds, finding her entrance and surging upward. My head fell back, a groan of pure animal pleasure erupting from me at the tight, hot feel. A moan of ecstasy melted from her luscious mouth.

Behind my closed eyes, brightness surged. I opened them to see that a light emitted from the rune stone behind us. Was the magic working? I didn't remember a light from before. Or it could have been my imagination, my need for it to happen. This was partially a dream after all.

I gripped her round hips, locked my eyes on hers and said, "I love ye so damn much."

Emma grinned down at me with an impish tilt to her lips. "Prove it. Worship me."

"Och, love, but I already do." I leaned up on my elbow, dragging her head toward me and claimed her mouth in a searing, tongue twisting kiss as I pumped my cock in and out of her. One hand threaded through her hair, tugging gently enough to cause a sting, the other held tight to her hips.

Emma rode me hard, her thighs clutched tight to my hips, her arse bouncing up and down on my thighs. She pressed her hands to my chest.

Good God, but she was amazing. The dream was so real, so filled with pleasure and bliss. Every bit as beautiful and memorable as real life.

As our bodies joined, and we made love the way we did best, I couldn't help but keep thinking, *this better work*. I wanted her back. Hell, the dream was fucking amazing, but Emma in the flesh... Having her with me day and night, that was the true miracle.

Her nails scraped over my shoulders, and suddenly she was pushing me backward, gripping my hands and thrusting them over my head. The temptress was back, her hips swiveling faster, harder. Her breasts bounced near my face. Close enough that if I leaned up, I might be able to grip one luscious nipple between my teeth. I tried, but missed her by half an inch.

I groaned, licked my lips and wished I were licking her flesh. Emma's blue eyes were still locked on mine, her pupils dilated, skin flushed, and a sexy smile curling her mouth. She liked to torment me.

Emma leaned forward enough to tease my mouth with her breasts, and I did my best to delight her with my roving tongue.

"Ye're amazing," I murmured.

"You're everything I ever wanted. Everything, Logan. I don't want to lose you."

I shook my head, tightening my hold on her hands over my head.

"Never. Ye'll never lose me, love."

"I'm so close," she murmured. "But I don't want to come. I'm afraid."

"Dinna be afraid of pleasure," I said, then had to grind my teeth because I was dangerously close to exploding and the way she was riding me, I'd be doing so any moment.

"I'm afraid it will wake us up."

The rune stone flickered, catching both of our attention. Emma's eyes met mine, worry filling her face. Her grip on my hands loosened. But I wouldn't let her, let go. I held on tight, and pumped my hips harder.

"Come, lass. Let yourself climax with me."

Her throat bobbed, and she nodded, relaxing a little, matching her rhythm to mine. I concentrated on her, working to give her pleasure until we were both shuddering, crying out, fiery release ripping through our beings so clearly and defined I thought it might have touched my soul.

Emma collapsed on top of me, our bodies slick with sweat, our breaths coming hard and fast.

She hugged me tight and I wrapped her up in my embrace, pressing my face to her hair and breathing her in.

"Do you think it worked?" she asked.

"Aye." But I wasn't certain. I didn't feel that magical tingling that I'd felt when I'd been in the torturer's chamber, that surge of power filling my limbs that had set me free.

I felt languid, blissfully happy with her lying in my arms, and yet sorrowful because I didn't know when she'd be taken from me again. I was terrified. A feeling completely foreign to me.

"Logan," she croaked, sitting up straight, eyes locked on mine and filled with fear. "I can feel myself drifting..."

Her body shimmered, flickered, and then was still again. I looked behind us, the rune stone's light fading.

I sat up with her, clutching her to me and kissing her. I would kiss her until she was no longer there.

"Stay, stay, stay," I chanted against her mouth.

"I want to." She held me tight, kissed me back just as hard.

But I could feel her fading, feel the press of her lips dissipate.

And then she was gone, and I was left clutching at air.

"Emma!" I leapt to my feet, turning in a circle, my skin, which had been so hot, suddenly cold. I tucked myself back into my breeches, and ran around the perimeter of the grove, praying she'd just decided to tease me. To hide for the fun of it.

I checked behind the stones; parted gorse bushes; looked behind trees.

But I was utterly alone.

And very awake. I didn't remember waking up. I didn't remember falling asleep either. Who knew what kind of state I'd been in, a fugue, but I was positive Emma had been there with me. I could still smell her. Still feel the heat of her touch on my skin. Hear her moans fill the air.

I glared up at the dark sky. Hours had passed since I'd first arrived. The moon shone overhead. The sacred rune stone in the middle of the grove was dark. The glow that had emanated from it when Emma had been here was completely gone. I jogged toward it, pressed my hands to its cold face and shuddered.

"What do I do?" I shouted at the sky. "How can I bring her back to me?"

But there was no answer.

Only mocking silence.

EMMA

I woke with a start, sitting straight up in a strange bed, sucking in air as though it were the last breath I'd ever take.

My hands pressed to my chest and I had to resist the intense urge to claw away the flesh and bone so I could breathe.

Where was I? What was happening?

I blinked, afraid and unnerved. But then, everything slowly came back to me. The time travel. Steven. Mrs. MacDonald.

My dream.

I slid my hands down over my legs, my skin cold to the touch. And yet, my body was still alive with tingles and shivers, scorched from making love with Logan.

Oh, how quick and cruel Fate had been to rip me away from him. The deep ache that had settled in my chest the moment I woke at Mrs. Lamb's to see Steven towering over me, returned with a vengeance.

The room was dark, chilly. I swung my legs over the side of the bed, smelling something delicious cooking downstairs.

Rather than enticing me though, the scent of the spices and onions turned my stomach. I felt hungover. Beat up. My head was still pounding, my limbs heavy and sluggish.

My bare toes touched the cold wood floor. I must have kicked off my shoes while I napped.

I rubbed at my temples, but that pressure didn't seem to alleviate the pounding in my skull even the tiniest bit.

The dream... It had been real.

I could still feel Logan's touch; the sizzle of his kiss, the excitement of being with him, the desperation as I'd slowly watched him fade away. How I'd tried to swim back through the ethereal tunnel I was being sucked back in.

Oh, I knew I hadn't been transported anywhere physically, but I'd been there all the same. Logan had been there. Just like years before. Our souls had found a place to meet. A place to beat Fate at her own game.

Was this a sign that Fate thought we belonged together? Had she allowed it to happen? Or was it only a sign that we were strong enough to force our spirits together and Fate had other plans? Finally gaining control when she brought me back here.

My mouth was dry, cottony. I stood up slowly, holding out my hands to steady myself, and then bent toward the floor, sliding my hands over the planks and beneath the bed until I found my shoes. I put them on, having forgotten the pinch in my toes. They weren't exactly my size. I made my way toward the door, fumbling in the shadowy dark for the handle, grateful for the small golden sliver of light from an outside lamppost shining through the blinds.

How long had I been asleep? Couldn't have been too long if Mrs. MacDonald was still cooking. I opened the door, and made my way toward the bathroom to splash water on my face.

Running water.

There had been a lot of adjustments I'd had to make living in the 1540's, things like plumbing, that I'd now taken advantage of several times since being back in the modern era.

The cool water slid over my skin, dripping from my chin onto the black, borrowed dress, and a shiver passed over me. I looked into the mirror, my red hair in disarray, having fallen from the tight bun I'd pulled it into at Mrs. MacDonald's house after my shower. Dark circles filled the space beneath my blue eyes. Eyes that looked faded in the flickering yellow light of the bathroom.

My skin was pale, jaundice almost from the light, but filled out, attesting to my usual health. I looked tired, though. And my face did not nearly give away the anguish that I felt.

I squeezed a glob of toothpaste onto my finger and rubbed it over my teeth, swishing with water. The mint was strong, bitingly so, compared with the tooth powder at Gealach.

With a long, drawn out sigh, I opened the bathroom door and eyed the narrow flight of stairs. I wanted to climb back into bed, but guilt at having left a perfect stranger, who'd done me the biggest of favors, alone for as long as I had already, ate at me. The least I could do was eat the meal she'd cooked and then go back to bed.

At the bottom of the stairs, voices floated from the kitchen and I froze. I couldn't hear what they were saying, but I could very distinctly hear the male undertones. And it wasn't the television. Because the responses came from Mrs. MacDonald.

Was it a trap?

Had she let Steven in?

I pressed my hand to the wall, bracing myself, and trying to draw an even breath. My feet were glued to the floor. I wasn't taking another step. I turned around, prepared to leave. To just walk out, even without the purse full of money that Mrs. Lamb had given me, which was upstairs where I'd left it.

Maybe somehow I could find a way to contact my Aunt Sheila back in the States. That was if she was still alive, or not on a bender. She'd never been reliable a day in my life. Why did I think now, when I'd need her most, that she would be?

I frowned. Didn't matter. I was going.

As soon as my palm touched the doorknob, Mrs. MacDonald called out, "Emma, dear, is that ye?"

I bit my lip hard enough to wince. Dammit. I turned the handle, prepared to make a run for it.

"Emma?"

I turned around, stiff and slow, to see Mrs. MacDonald and an older gentleman standing right behind me in the archway toward the kitchen.

"Where are ye going?" Mrs. MacDonald asked, wiping her hands on a kitchen towel, her expression concerned.

The man beside her had a full head of graying hair. His face was clean-shaven; wrinkles lined his eyes and mouth. He wore a dark suit, navy blue or gray. I couldn't tell in the light. He looked like a businessman, but not one of those I'd seen Steven meet with when we'd vacationed in Scotland.

I didn't recognize the man from anywhere, and yet, the way he looked at me, was as if he knew who I was.

Perhaps he was a friend of Mrs. MacDonald's that she'd called to keep her company while I napped. Maybe she'd told him about me, and that was why he looked at me so familiarly.

"I need some air," I managed to say.

"There's a lovely patio in the back," Mrs. MacDonald said, hooking her thumb over her shoulder. "More private."

Concealed is what she meant. No one, including Steven, would see me, and that must mean the man with her was a good friend—else why would she suggest it and he be nodding his agreement?

"All right, "I said, walking toward them, and they backed up to allow me to pass. But I stopped halfway down the corridor, and eyed the man. "I'm sorry, who are you?"

He grinned, gazing at me knowingly. "Apologies for not introducing myself earlier. I'm Shona and Moira's guardian, Albert McAlister."

"Guardian?" I winged a brow, keeping myself still though I wanted to take a step backward. "They are well past the age in which they need a guardian."

Who was this guy? How had he convinced Mrs. MacDonald to let him in? The old woman gazed at him, nodding. What the hell? Had he somehow drugged her?

Albert McAlister chuckled. "Not that type of guardian. I was appointed to keep watch over them and their estate when they were children. I have continued to do so in their adulthood. I'm their solicitor."

"Ah." A lawyer, a financier. I didn't completely understand, and the way he glanced at me, I was certain he had some questions—such as, where were Moira and Shona?

I cleared my throat, hoping we could just move past that part. "If you'll excuse me," I said, walking past them and out the sliding glass door at the rear of the house.

Mr. McAlister gave me a look that said we weren't finished, and I didn't doubt it. I was just glad he didn't follow me outside.

The cool blast of autumn evening air felt marvelous on my skin, which had gone from cold to hot upon seeing the man with Mrs. MacDonald.

I moved out to the small grassy area of the yard. The plants in the rear were also drooping, as had the ones in front. If McAlister was the one to have taken care of the inside of the house, as it seemed someone had, then he'd also been the one to let the front and back go to crap.

I don't know why I found that to be so offensive. Maybe it was because Moira and Shona both had amazing skills with plants. And didn't they own an herbal shop here? Shona took such pride with the gardens at Gealach. I think she'd be heartbroken if she saw the state of things in her own backyard.

The air suddenly felt too constrictive. I turned around and went back inside. The need to yell or scream or stomp or *something* burned within me.

I stared Mr. McAlister right in the eye, Mistress of Castle Gealach taking front and center to all the miserable shit I'd been put through in the past dozen hours. I stabbed my finger toward him, then at the glass door.

"If you are supposed to take care of their estate, you've done a poor job of keeping up with their property."

He glanced around taking in the interior of the house, and I shook my head.

"Moira and Shona are exceedingly proud of their green thumbs. They'd never leave their yard to ruin."

Mr. McAlister's mouth fell open, he looked surprised.

"And I would think as their *guardian,* you would know such a thing." I crossed my arms defensively over my chest, suddenly unsure exactly where I stood with these people.

If I'd been able to travel back and forth in time, who was to say they hadn't done that very same thing themselves?

Perhaps the fact that I was standing before a MacDonald wasn't a coincidence after all.

My blood ran cold. God, how I wished Logan was here to give me strength.

"My dear," Mrs. MacDonald said, a questionable light coming into her eyes, her mouth parting in shock. She wrung her hands and looked back and forth between the both of us. "We are both here to help ye."

I cocked my head studying her. I wanted to believe her, what reason did she have to lie—other than the fact that she could very well be my enemy?

I suppressed a shudder, recalling to mind the image of Laird MacDonald standing in our great hall. The vicious look in his eyes, the venomous words.

"I'm not certain I can believe you," I said.

Mr. McAlister held out his hands in surrender. "I understand your situation is a bit frightening."

"What do you know of my situation?" I asked, interrupting.

Did they know *all* of it? Or just what Mrs. Lamb would have relayed about me running away from Steven? Mrs. MacDonald had not questioned my attire, though she had to have taken note that I was not dressed in modern day clothes when she called me into her house. Then again, she could have simply guessed that Steven made me dress that way. One never knew when it came to controlling men what exactly they would have their wives do.

Or maybe she'd just assumed that it was a cultural or religious decision. I'd seen that before.

"I know ye're a friend of Shona and Moira's." His eyes were honest as he met mine, nodding slowly as if hoping to subtly convey that he wanted my agreement.

I narrowed my eyes.

"I came by the house to check and see if they'd yet arrived. I come by every day around this same time, usually when I'm finished at my office. I keep their place stocked with food. There is a cleaning lady that comes once a week to make certain the house doesn't fill with dust in their absence." He shook his head, looking slightly ashamed. "I'd not thought about the yard, which I should have, and I appreciate ye pointing out my shortcomings there." He stuck his hand in his pocket and I winced, expecting to see him pull out a weapon despite his convincing words, but all he did was pull out his cell phone.

"What are you doing with that?" I asked, picturing the man signaling to Steven that he had me and then watching my ex-husband storm through the door.

We might still legally be married in Steven's eyes, and perhaps even the eyes of the law, but to me, he was a stranger. My ex. Never would I allow him control over me again.

I'd been gone for years, divorced him in my mind and moved on.

I was Logan's wife. In love with Logan. We had a child.

But I was more than that; I was also my own person. Steven had never wanted me to be anything more than a possession. A robot. A plaything.

I couldn't belong to Steven anymore. A plaything that he kept locked up and only let out when he wanted to jab at me with his words or body.

"I'm going to call the shop. There's a lass there who works for Shona and Moira, been running it since they left. She'll know best what to do about the yard. I admit to knowing next to nothing about keeping plants."

I didn't know what to say. I had no way of proving whether or not these people were actually helping me or hindering me. The best I could do was stay on my toes. Not let my guard down.

"How about some supper?" Mrs. MacDonald asked, breaking the silence.

"It smells delicious," Mr. McAlister said.

My stomach grumbled, but I still felt too jumpy to eat a thing, afraid it would all come right back up.

"How about a glass of wine?" he asked me, walking toward

the counter. He lifted a bottle of red. "I brought this in hopes Moira would be home. She has great taste in wine."

"When was the last time you talked to either of them?" I asked.

He let out a long sigh. "I've not seen or spoken to Shona in years." He eyed me, perhaps trying to decipher how much I knew. "Moira says she ran off with a man."

Moira had spent the last few years before coming to 1544 thinking her sister had gone missing—coincidentally at the same time Rory had also gone missing. No one had been able to find her; the authorities had labeled her disappearance a cold case.

I nodded, not wanting to give away that up until now, I'd been living with Shona at Castle Gealach.

"And Moira?" I asked.

"She's been gone just a couple weeks now."

Long enough for her plants to die, but not long enough for anyone to really take note? Except the neighbor...

"Did you alert the authorities?" I asked.

Mr. McAlister sighed again, rifling through a drawer to find a wine opener and Mrs. MacDonald stared at him, willing him to say yes, I supposed.

"She's not missing," he finally answered, peeling the foil from around the top of the bottle and screwing the opener into the cork.

"Then where is she?" Mrs. MacDonald asked, her hand fluttering to her throat, the spoon left dipped into the pot, all thoughts of serving dinner gone.

The cork popped from the bottle and Mr. McAlister stared me right in the eye, a knowing look. He grinned and said, "Emma knows."

6

LOGAN

The woods echoed with night sounds. Creaks and howls, chirps and buzzes. A warm breeze blew around my ankles, covered in a mist that glowed from the light of the moon.

My body still stirred with the memory of my wife, her touch, and her kiss.

Mo chreach, I missed her with a fierce passion.

Appearing to me in the glen had been real. I'd never fallen asleep, and I was fairly certain I wasn't hallucinating.

My boots crunched roughly over the forest floor, disturbing small creatures that scurried to hide. I cared not who heard me. Nor did I care if I woke any of my enemies who lay in wait for just such an opportunity.

In fact, I welcomed anyone to dare tempt me into battle. I couldn't wait to unleash the fury that drove me forward.

I had enough anger swirling with the ache in my veins that I was likely to murder a man with my bare hands should he leap in front of me.

Down the mountain I stormed, toward the loch at the bottom. Hacking at tree branches, overgrown weeds that stuck onto my breeches like tiny, clinging fingers of irritation.

I broke through the trees, the loch gently lapping at the shore, mocking me with its peaceful sound.

A beam of moonlight shone on my rowboat, beckoning me to climb back in. But I didn't want to.

I stood staring at my castle across the water. The turrets jutting from one end of the sky to the other. The walls were high, thick. Torches blazed along the walls. The moon shone on the irons spikes of the portcullis. The structure was fortified to an extreme. No sane man would dare scale its walls or attempt to breach its gates, unless death was what he wished for.

And yet, Fate had been able to easily take siege of Gealach. Fate had me by the ballocks. Twisted into knots.

For a man who prided himself on control, on power, I was unnerved.

Unraveled.

My gaze roved to the ships, large and imposing as they rocked in the gentle current. A mix of our own, and some we'd commandeered. They loomed from the docks like monsters in the dark. Well-built warships, almost ancient in appearance with their swooping Viking design and dragon bows. But the wood was new. Polished, cared for. The design was meant to entice fear—to bring out the memories of Vikings invading these lands. To exploit images of them ravishing the women, annihilating the men, enslaving the children.

And it worked.

That was why the new king, and the old, had trusted me as the guardian. The one who could keep him on the throne.

Even though it could have been mine. Everything. I didn't want it—a notion that shocked most. But not Emma. She knew me inside and out.

I kicked the boat toward the shore. Still full of fury. The pound of my foot and scrape of the boat's bottom masked the night sounds of bugs and animals.

All was silent on the wall across the way, patrolled by a few guards who remained hidden from those who might wish to attempt a siege.

And I was suddenly enraged at the injustice of this. That my wife should be missing, taken from me by the whim of Fate, and the world did not rage with me. The world was silent, sleeping, unknowing of my pain.

I fisted my hands at my sides, let my head fall back and a bellow loud enough to make the trees and ground shudder, erupted from my throat.

"Why?" I shouted.

Forget the boat.

I needed the cold of the loch sluicing over my skin, to calm me. I couldn't return to the castle like this. I was ill composed, and of such a mind, my men would likely think I'd lost all sense and reason. I stripped, tossing my things into the rowboat that was moored up on the shore, and dove in.

The loch was frigid and churned with the same ferocity I felt. How many times had I used the loch and her angry current to battle the demons inside? To freeze the fiery anger? To work out the madness? An ire that had been present, before Emma, before she'd healed me, made me whole, found a crack in my fortitude and crept back in, causing me to feel as though I were balancing on the edge of a sword's blade. Since I could remember, night swimming was routine for me. Nearly daily, even when snow fell upon my head and chunks of ice floated past. The cold focused me. Helped me to think, to work through whatever issue needed deciphering.

There was no ice now. The water was almost pleasant,

allowing me more energy to think than to concentrate on staying warm.

But how could I think my way through this situation? Fate had stolen my wife from me. There was no way to grasp hold, to control the outcome.

I dove deeper, letting the cooler temperatures of the deeper water sink into my skin, down to my bones. This time, the water did nothing to quell the heat that raged in my veins.

God, I wanted her back. Needed her.

My life had been so different before she'd appeared. So lacking. I'd been on a downward spiral with no coming back, until she'd steadied me.

Emma.

I still remembered vividly the very first time I'd seen her, tumbling backward, end over end, long, shapely legs exposed. Her modern blouse stretched across her breasts—at the time I'd had no idea my wife had come from another time. She was simply an enigma. A unicorn. A thing of beauty thrust into a world of darkness and gore. She'd looked up at me with her large, almond-shaped blue eyes. Eyes that I looked into every morning since. Seductive eyes. Soulful eyes. When she looked at me, even now, I felt as though she saw right inside me, to the very core of my darkest secrets. But even knowing what those deep, dark secrets were, she'd not run away, she'd let me take her hand in mine. Let me touch her. Let me breathe in her sweet scent. Let me love her. Marry her. Create a child with her. Our son.

Soul mates, we were.

And now Fate was trying to rip her from me—had done so, in fact.

Kicking harder, arms pulling me deeper in a routine as familiar as my wife's face, I touched the bottom, before shooting back to the top, lungs burning for a breath of air.

Finally, I burst upon the surface, taking that much-needed gulp, flicking wet hair from my face.

The mountain that housed the stone circle jutted upward before me, the castle was at my back. Trees swayed in the breeze and the moon lit a path to the very top, to the glen, where I'd made love to my wife not an hour before.

I could still see her rising over me. Eyes hooded with desire, teeth biting her lower lip, creamy skin glowing with perspiration.

"Where are ye, Emma? When will ye come back to me?"

I smoothed away the water that dripped into my eyes. There had only been a few times in my life that I felt emotional enough to be brought to tears, and knowing for certain now, that Emma was no longer here, that brought me to my knees. I shuddered. 'Twas time to head back to shore. To take the boat back to Castle Gealach. To speak with Ewan about what I knew now to be a certainty.

She was in another time. Another world that I couldn't reach. A place I'd never been, nor could fathom. Aye, she'd told me stories of her world. Of the modernizations I couldn't comprehend. The values, the politics. None of it seemed real, most of it I couldn't imagine. How had she survived in a world like that? How had any of them?

'Twas a miracle the earth still existed with the weapons she said they used. The way they could travel by air from one place to the next, a speed at which I could barely grasp.

We lived so much more simply here. And yet, infinitely more complicated.

I pulled my arms through the water, rotating my shoulders, twisting from side to side, legs kicking powerfully. Every stroke, every kick, was me pounding Fate into bloody submission. At least, for my own sanity.

When I reached the shore, dripping wet, I didn't bother to dress. I simply yanked the boat back into the water, and hopped in. By the time I reached the shore, I was dry enough to put on my breeches.

Ewan approached from out of the dark. His feet silent on the grass and sand.

I glanced at him, his face tight as he watched me.

"She is gone," Ewan said, not asking, but knowing.

"Aye." Admitting it was painful, as though I were realizing it all over again for the first time. "But she'll be coming back. I'm going to make damn sure of it."

Ewan nodded, his support a great comfort to me. Emma was his sister. The man would want her back almost as much as I did.

"Did ye see her?" he asked.

"Aye." I raked my hand through my wet hair.

Ewan tugged my boat up further onto the shore. "The glen has magic. Shona and I went back to modern day when we were together by the stone."

I knew this story. I'd heard it a dozen times. When the six of us, Emma, me, Ewan, Shona, Moira and Rory, were together, we often talked about time travel. I was the only one of the six who'd not yet traveled, or "journeyed" as Rory liked to say. I didn't feel left out by that fact, quite the contrary. I was blessed to still be here. Or at least, that was what I'd always thought until now.

Och, what I wouldn't give to scoop up Saor and blend in with the mist, walking out of it into the arms of Emma in whatever world she was in. I'd brave that mad modern realm, if I could only be with her.

"If there is one thing we've learned, my laird, 'tis that ye'll see her again."

I frowned. "But that could be years, and there is no guarantee." Rory had been missing for nearly five years by the time he'd returned. Ewan had come to the Highlands as a boy, and not returned to modern times until just the past year, and only for a few short hours at that.

"I canna live without her," I said. "I dinna *want* to live without her."

"I know how ye feel, Logan." Ewan patted me awkwardly on my bare shoulder. "But we must remain positive, else, Fate will have won. Ye've a son to care for, a clan that depends on ye, and a country that has named ye its guardian. Fight on, Logan. Dinna give up."

I stared up at the sky, willing it to open up, to strike me down with a lightning bolt. "Why did she bring this battle to me? I dinna think I am strong enough to withstand the pain."

"I dinna know why she chose ye. But I do know ye are strong enough. Ye've faced far worse. I know it doesna seem that way to ye, but it's true."

I only glared at him. There was nothing worse than losing the love of my life.

"I think we'd best send for Rory and Moira," Ewan said. "We need them."

"Aye." I agreed, though I couldn't fathom what good it would do.

"'Haps, with all of us together, we can somehow bring her back." Ewan shrugged, his face clouded.

"I will try anything." We trudged up the slippery water gate stairs toward the outer bailey. Ewan told the guard at the top to secure the rowboat.

By now many had roused, and stared at me with faces full of concern.

The clan, my lands, Scotland—*my son*—were at a disadvantage. With my mind split between worry for Emma and duties to the clan, an enemy could sneak up behind me and I'd only notice maybe half the time.

I regarded those in the bailey, their eyes still filled with sleep. They looked at me as though waiting for answers I didn't have to give. They didn't know about time travel, and I couldn't tell them without them all thinking I was mad. They would assume the enemy had taken Emma, and that we should be calling for war against whoever that enemy was.

And even though it felt that way, as though she'd been yanked right from my arms, she'd not been taken by an enemy with a face. Or one we knew by name. One we could bring our swords down upon to show our superior might.

How in holy hell was I going to explain it?

"Your mistress has gone missing," I said, wincing at the gasps that went up through the people, the soft murmurs that moved in waves. "But we will do everything we can to find her."

"Do ye know who took her?" one of the guards that had been at the bottom of the stairs asked.

I shook my head. The man was likely wracking his brain, trying to figure out how the enemy could have gotten past him.

I would have liked to ease his mind, to let him know he wasn't going crazy, anymore than I was, but there was nothing I could say to ease those fears. Nothing that would make sense to him.

Ballocks!

Just then, Shona rushed from the castle, her face pale, eyes wide, and hair in disarray. She looked from Ewan to me, and back again, her mouth forming an O of surprise.

"Emma..." she started to say but trailed off.

Ewan walked toward her with wide steps, pulling her into his embrace and whispering something against her ear. The show of affection, the comfort they sought from each other, only brought me pain. I winced and looked away.

I needed a drink. A strong one. My legs felt heavy as I lifted them, taking one step at time until I could reach the castle, when what I really wanted to do was set up camp in the glen and pray that my wife returned to me.

What I wouldn't give to have her back. I'd give up Gealach, my position as the king's servant. I'd live as an outlaw the rest of my days if only I could have her back.

And even as I thought it, I could see her frown. See her wag her finger at me when she didn't like what I was doing. She'd not want me to give it up. She'd want our son provided for. But didn't she understand? Didn't she know how very much I depended on her? I had not lived before she came into my life, merely existed.

I didn't bother with the great hall but headed straight to my library, opening the door with enough force to cause it to slam into the wall, disrupting a painting that Emma had placed there the previous year. 'Twas a picture of us both, one that had been commissioned shortly after our wedding.

She said it was tradition to have a portrait done of a wedded couple where she was from, and I'd agreed, though I wondered if the reason she'd wanted it now was so that I had something to look upon when she disappeared. A piece of evidence that she was real.

I studied the painting of us both. The artist had captured the excitement in our eyes, our love. The secret curl of our lips. She looked like a red-haired angel, and I the devil who'd caught her. Her hand was reaching across my middle, touching my sword, and one of my arms was around her, the other touching her elbow, as though I were leading that arm to my sword.

That was a telling sign; a show to any who would look that Emma wasn't just my wife. She was my partner. My other half. Her disappearance left a gaping wound in my chest.

I turned from the painting and headed to the sideboard. Pouring more than a few drams of whisky into my cup. I needed it. Needed to feel the burn of liquor sloshing down my throat.

After downing the entire cup's contents, I considered refilling, or perhaps simply drinking from the jug, to feel nothing. To bring on the numbness that such quantities of liquor would afford me.

But I didn't. Instead, I whipped toward the hearth and hurled the cup into its barren black mouth.

The mug clattered against the stone, but didn't shatter, for it was made of metal, and even as angry as I was, as much as I needed to destroy something, I couldn't make metal break.

"I've sent a messenger," Ewan said from behind me.

I couldn't look at him. Couldn't turn around. My breaths were heavy, my heart pounding. I didn't want him to see my pain, to know for a fact that my heart was rupturing. That I was weak after all.

"Tell me when they arrive. Now, leave me."

Ewan muttered something and backed out of the room, shutting the door behind him.

I picked up the jug of whisky and whipped it toward the hearth. Constructed from earthenware material, it did shatter into a hundred jagged shards.

But instead of feeling satisfied, I was only filled with frustration.

7

MOIRA

I basked in sublime pleasure. What naughtiness we got away with in the year 1544 was completely different than had the date been of a modern era...

Rory was supposed to be working.

He was supposed to be occupied with his lairdly documents, and then there was the usual training of his men.

But I'd kept him from leaving our bedroom.

And he couldn't get fired for being late because he was the one in charge.

His head rose, lips glistening, from between my thighs, where he'd licked and sucked until I came so hard, my hips literally bucked from the bed.

Damn, but he was good at that.

I stretched lazily, my legs still spread wide for his viewing pleasure.

"That was... so good," I murmured.

"I'm not done with ye yet," he growled, climbing up over my body, hands at my sides, thighs settling between mine.

His muscles shimmered with sweat, and his smile... God, but his smile could melt ice.

My body vibrated from the sheer power of him, the raw sexuality that oozed from every pore. Oh, yes, I'd just come, but the sight of him made me ready to do so all over again.

I shuddered, my clit still pulsing from his tongue, and anticipating what was coming next.

He gripped one of my thighs and tugged upward until I lengthened my leg out, my foot resting on his shoulder. He kissed my ankle, scraped his teeth over the arch of my foot. I shivered.

"But, your men, they are waiting for you," I teased, grinning, and knowing he'd not be leaving this room until he'd left me spent on the bed.

What Rory liked to do was make me come over and over. He liked to watch me orgasm, to see me walk a little slower than normal because my thighs ached from being spread so long.

And, let's be honest, I liked it, too.

We'd been at Dunleod Castle just a few months. Ranulf, my stepson—God, that was weird to say—was still here at the castle with us. He'd just turned twenty years old, and was still acting like a complete dick. A spoiled, vindictive little asshole.

Rory took him daily from his locked chamber out to the field, trained him with the rest of his men, even let him eat in the great hall—which was a good thing. His son shouldn't be kept a prisoner, but I guess it was needed considering Ranulf threatened at least once a week to gut Rory and to tie me naked to a pike and burn me.

But why was I thinking about that now? What a mood killer.

I shook away the tedious and mundane, concentrating on Rory's tongue sliding down my calf.

"How do ye want it?" he asked, wiggling his brows with wicked intent.

"Anyway you want to give it to me," I said, biting my lip. I reached to trail my fingers over one thick pectoral, down the ridges of his abdomen, brushing through the tuft of hair at the base of his thick cock.

I wrapped my fingers around his warm, velvet shaft, feeling it jump in my hand. Hot damn, but every time I touched him, I still had a hard time believing he, this, us, was a reality. When we'd first dated years ago, in the modern world, I'd thought I must have been dreaming. A guy like him, wanting a girl like me? It wasn't that I didn't have confidence in myself, well, maybe a slight touch of self-esteem had been nicked, but he was so freaking hot, he could have had any woman he wanted, and he chose me. A nerdy, history-loving, herbalist.

For goodness' sake, he'd traveled five hundred years in the future—*twice*—to find me. Thank god, I'd been able to go back with him the second time.

I loved him so much, I couldn't imagine living without him. If he'd disappeared again... Ugh. I didn't even want to think about it. Or the man I'd taken up with after he left the first time. Dickie was a real *winner*—sarcasm intentional.

"I want ye..." He drawled out the *ye* and glanced around the room.

We'd made love on every surface and against every square inch of floor and wall. Where could he possibly take me that we hadn't already explored? Who was I kidding? I didn't care where, as long as he thrust inside me soon.

"Come with me." He leapt from the bed, his cock bouncing against his thighs, and pulled me up. "I want to try something different."

Different had been the name of the game lately. We'd had time to play without me getting pregnant. Some years back, I'd opted for a birth control shot versus an IUD... Thank god, because if I'd gotten the IUD, there was no telling how the hell I'd get it out. It wasn't like I could request Fate send me back for my yearly gynecological appointment. My last shot had been about a week before Rory came back to the modern era. Since I was supposed to repeat the shots every three months to avoid pregnancy, I figured it had worn off about a month ago. My periods had stopped a while ago with the shot, and had yet to restart. I didn't even know if I'd get one between now and getting pregnant. I secretly hoped to avoid one altogether. Selfish, maybe, but periods were the worst. The cramping, the mess... Not to mention the lack of tampons.

Emma and Shona had filled me in on what it was like to have a period in 1544 and it sounded like a nightmare. I think I could make my excuses to Rory and stay in bed the entire five to seven days it took to run its course. With only a wad of fabric to collect anything... Ick. Who wouldn't stay in bed?

I could see some men thinking that having a period was a woman's excuse to be lazy for a week, but, a man had never had cramps, or any of the other gross things attached to it.

And once again, why was I thinking about that now?

Rory slapped my arse, a wakeup call. I cried out, a little startled, and he chuckled.

"Welcome back, love."

He set me on my feet, bending low for a minute to flick his tongue over my nipple, his hands cupping my breasts. Oh, yes, this...

"There's something I've always wanted to try," he said.

"I'm willing to try anything," I murmured, threading my hands through his hair and moaning.

"I love that about ye," he said. "Wait right here."

"Trust me, I'm not going anywhere."

I watched him walk, naked, toward the foot of our bed. His ass was pure sexual perfection. Muscular, round, and just as tanned as the rest of him. He swam naked regularly, and I'd joined him on several occasions, though my pale skin had ended up burned, while his turned a delicious golden brown.

Rory opened the trunk at the foot of the bed and pulled out a small satchel. He wiggled his brows at me, and then tugged open the strings and pulled out a long stretch of silky-looking cord.

"What's that?" I asked.

"A gift from Logan."

I winged a brow.

"A wedding gift," he said, a naughty curve to his lips.

My brow rose even further. I knew men in the modern era liked to talk shop, but I hadn't realized they would in the past. They were all big, strong and warrior-like, talking politics and battle strategy.

But sex?

I guess I was wrong.

"What's it for?" I asked, curious. Was he going to tie me up? "And why haven't we used it sooner?"

"Ye'll see... And I was waiting for just the right moment. This seems like it."

Rory looked around the room and then settled on a metal hook in the wall that had held a tapestry I'd asked him to remove it because it creeped me out. A battle scene that was gory in its threaded detail didn't exactly help me to fall asleep at night.

At his tall height, Rory easily reached the hook and threaded the cord through it, making a whizzing sound as he did it.

"Come here," he said, crooking his finger at me.

I complied without question, bare feet padding across the cold stone. Eyes focused on him. My body was covered in tingles of anticipation.

"Face the wall and hold your hands up."

I did as he asked, pressing my fingers to the cold stone. I

arched my back a little, trying to get close to him. Wanting him to look at me and the curve of my back that led to my ass. Rory let out an appreciative whistle, sliding his hands over my buttocks, smacking one side and then the other.

"Have I told ye today how beautiful ye are?" He whispered in my ear, sliding the cord gently around my wrists, his hard cock pressing up against my rear, his breath on my neck.

"Only a dozen times," I murmured, body lighting on fire.

"Does that hurt?" he asked, tightening the cord.

"No." My heart pounded, breaths came quick. Excitement filled my blood. I'd never been tied up before, and the loss of control, of my husband being able to do whatever he wanted to me only made it that much more erotic.

From behind, Rory slid his hands up and down my sides, his knuckles scraping over my ribs, the tops of his nails skimming over the sides of my breasts. Gooseflesh rose in the wake of his touch, and I shuddered, excited and filled with eagerness.

He moved my hair to the side and pressed his lips to the skin at the nape of my neck. Rory glided his lips down over my spine, kneeling behind me to kiss each cheek of my behind. He used his hands to apply pressure to my legs, and I spread them, feeling the wetness of my need drip down the sides of my inner thighs.

His teeth skimmed over my thigh and then he was standing again, his fingers trailing over the places he'd kissed

"I still canna believe ye're here with me," he whispered.

"If it's a dream, I never want to wake."

He chuckled. "Then it's a good thing we seem to rarely leave our bed."

I started to giggle, but his hands skimmed around the front of my body, fingers sliding between my folds and circling over my clit. Oh, but he always knew just how to touch me.

My head fell back, and his mouth was waiting for me, his tongue diving deep to mix with mine. Rory could kiss me until my breath ceased. He was an expert kisser, from every angle, position... I moaned, arching my back so my buttocks reared against his engorged cock.

"How long will you make me wait?" I asked.

"Hours," he murmured. "Maybe I'll leave ye tied here all day. Return to ye every hour and make ye climax until ye collapse."

Was he serious? I'd be lying if I didn't admit the idea was more than intriguing. I shuddered, my nipples tightening, my sex throbbing, imagining myself helpless, wanting.

Rory sensed my reaction, and let out soft, gravelly laugh of satisfaction as he pinched my rear.

"Naughty, lass. Ye want me to do that..."

"Kind of," I said with a giggle.

He let out his breath in a long whistle, and then murmured. "I could tell the servants ye are ill, to leave ye be, then no one would come inside." He slid his hands up and over my forearms, gripping the backs of my hands where I held tight to the cord.

His cock seemed to grow behind me, pressing thick against my buttocks, and I reacted immediately, pushing back, wanting.

"Yes," I murmured.

"*Mo chreach*," he cursed in Gaelic. "What am I going to do with ye?"

I arched my back again, close enough that with one small twist, I could run my tongue over his lips. "Everything."

Rory groaned, opened his mouth and bit the tip of my tongue. "Damn, lass, but ye make me so hard. I'm going to walk around with my plaid tented the rest of the day."

A throaty laugh escaped me. "If you're going to leave me

tied here for hours... Well, then ye can think about that. About how much you want me."

Rory groaned. "Now who is being tormented?"

And then he was grabbing my hips, tugging me back, his cock notching at the entrance to my sex, and thrusting forward.

I cried out in surprise and pleasure, while he growled with feral passion.

"I'm going to tie ye to the bed, and keep ye there for all time." He thrust deep. Pulled out softly, and thrust deep again. "I want ye limp and wet and tingling all over."

I already was, holding tight to the cord as he drove deeper and deeper. My head had fallen back and all I could do was gasp and mewl.

He lifted me slightly, until I stood on my tiptoes, letting him push deeper inside me. Then, effortlessly, he lifted me all the way, and I held tight to the cord, my entire body vibrating from pleasure.

He pulled out, whirled me around, spreading my thighs around his hips and plunged in again. I held tight to him with my thighs, and he walked me backward, pressing my spine up against the wall.

"I like this cord," he said.

I could only reply in a moan as the pressure he created between my thighs sent bolts of fiery pleasure rocketing through my veins, my muscles, and my nerves. Everything was on fire with delicious sensation.

Rory claimed my mouth with his. I wanted badly to grab hold of him, to run my fingers through his hair. To tug on his locks enough to cause a spark of pain. To rake my nails down his back. To grab hold of that luscious ass and sink my fingers into his flesh. I was at his mercy, holding tight to the silky cord and squeezing his hips with my thighs, and kissing him with everything I had—which was harder than I thought considering the pleasure flashing within me.

He nibbled my lips, scraped his cheek over mine, and bit my earlobe, murmuring, "God, ye're incredible, *mo chridhe*."

Just the words, the simple expression of enjoyment and pride set my fire to an even greater inferno.

He pounded harder, our skin making smacking sounds that echoed against the stone. Our moans whirled in the rafters and I was certain everyone within all of Dunleod knew exactly what we were doing, and that thought only sent my pleasure to greater heights.

Rory gripped my buttocks. Our skin was slick, covered with a sheen of perspiration and mingling with the wetness of my sex.

He bit my shoulder, licking and kissing then biting again.

I was on the edge of a climax, my body singing for release. "I'm so close," I groaned, rocking my hips in time with his thrusts.

"I've half a mind to leave ye wanting," he growled. "To let ye hang here, body on fire. Yearning for me to return to finish ye off."

"No, no, no," I begged. "Dinna leave me like that. I'll go mad."

Rory chuckled, and ceased his thrusts. Pressing his hips tight to mine, my buttocks flush to the stone wall. Insides pulsing.

"Just like this," he said, hooded eyes meeting mine. "*Allll* day."

I imagined it then. Me, tied to the bed in desperate need of his hands, mouth and cock. That wouldn't do. Not without coming first.

I clenched the muscles of my vagina, gripping his cock inside me. "Two can play the game of torment."

"Fuck," he cursed, his forehead pressed to mine. "I canna.

I canna stop..." And then he was pounding into me. Hard. Fast. A wild, primal warrior.

All of my muscles tightened, anticipating what was to come—*me*.

I cried out as pleasure rocked me, jolting me from reality and into a world that only existed between the two of us.

Rory pressed me to the stone in earnest now, pounding deep inside me, his lips on my neck, hands on my ass, and then, he, too, was orgasming, the heat of his emission searing my insides.

Utterly limp, he untied me and carried me to the bed, where he tied my legs, spread wide, but left my hands free. I was still trembling.

"Why did you leave my hands free?" I asked.

He chuckled and winked. "Och, love. What ye could do with those hands..." Rory winked, then kissed me hard and deep until I was panting and trying to get him to climb into bed with me once more.

"Soon, love," he said. "I will not be able to get a lick of work done knowing ye're tied up here waiting for me. Pleasuring yourself..." His eyes slid to my parted thighs and the pink, wetness of my sex. "And this..." He slid a finger over me, making me jump. "I'll be lucky to make it a quarter of an hour before I'm back."

❧ 8 ❧

RORY

I made it *two* quarters of an hour, thirty minutes to be exact, before my cock rose to an excruciating point and images of Moira strapped to the bed refused to leave my mind.

What the hell was I doing down here anyway, going over ledgers again? It was a task that needed to be done, but who was I really tormenting? My wife, or myself?

Me thinks it was the latter, for I was burning with desire, need. Potent and harassing. When I checked the grain stores for winter, I saw the ties around the sacks, and all I could think about was the ties around her ankles. How she'd looked suspended from the cord in the ceiling, her legs wrapped around me, passion suffusing her flesh with a pink glow.

Aye, I needed to get back to her, and this time when I left her, I think I'd have to cry mercy, for I'd get no more work done knowing that she was laying up there waiting for me.

I let out a groan and slammed the papers down, marching toward the door with a single, sexual purpose in mind. Och, I was going to make love to her until neither of us could stand.

Have our noon meal served in our chamber, maybe supper, too.

But when I opened the door, a guard stood poised to knock. The only person I *wanted* to see standing in my way was Moira—naked—not the guard who actually inhabited the space.

"What do ye want?" I growled.

He cleared his throat and shifted once on his feet. "There's a messenger in the bailey for ye, my laird."

I drew in a long breath of air and let it out in a rush, several thoughts going through my mind. One, I could simply tell the guard to bugger off and that I was busy, the messenger be damned. Two, I could tell him to get the messenger a hot meal until I was ready. Or three, I could just deal with the messenger now, no matter how irritating it would be given my cock was hard as the stone walls.

If I went with one, it wouldn't bode well for the reputation I was trying hard to maintain within the clan. As it was, they'd been very patient with Moira and I, and our... bedchamber pursuits. And it would only feed Ranulf's displeasure that I was his sire and the many reasons in which he should be let loose to wreak havoc once again. That was something I could not abide by.

If I went with two, I'd be distracted when I was with Moira, and that was the last thing I wanted when she was so eager to give and receive pleasure. Thinking about the messenger when I was with my wife was out of the question.

Bloody hell. Option three it was.

Mayhap the fresh air would do me good.

And, mayhap, upstairs, my wife was doing something altogether naughty. I wouldn't want to interrupt her from that. Dammit, I actually would...

I grunted to the guard and pushed past him toward the main doors, shoving them open a little more forcefully than was necessary. I stood at the top of the keep stairs, glowering at the messenger who stood nervously in the bailey, the reins of his horse still in his hands, though he stood beside it. He looked to be about the same age as my son, and he was covered in a film of dirt and grime. I could smell his stench from where I stood. Either he was not very good at personal hygiene, or he'd ridden hard and fast to reach me.

"My laird," he said before I'd addressed him.

My glower deepened, but he didn't stop speaking, only attesting to his urgent message.

"Apologies, but ye must come quick. The Guardian, he needs ye." The messenger met my gaze, pleading in his eyes.

The Guardian. Logan Grant. If he was summoning me, then it must be dire.

"What's it in regards to?" I asked in the hopes the man had an idea.

"Your wife is also to come." The messenger shook his head, slapped the side of it. "The lady, our mistress, she is missing."

That one word, *missing*, had the ability to drain all the blood from my body, leaving it to pool in my boots, and I feared I'd sweat it right out of the bottom of my feet.

"Missing? What do ye know of this?"

"Not much. The laird woke in the night to find her gone. They searched the castle and surrounding grounds for hours and there is no sign of her."

Ballocks!

Nay!

The very thing I feared myself... Moira going back to the future. I'd been back and forth; there was no telling when it would happen.

Had Emma been taken back? The messenger wouldn't have that answer, but Logan might.

"Do they know who took her?" I asked, just in case.

The messenger shook his head. "Not a clue, my laird. Not one clue. 'Tis as if she vanished into thin air."

Mo chreach... 'Twas true.

"Get a meal, refresh your horse. We will pack and leave within the hour."

The messenger thanked me. He handed his mount off to one of our stable lads, and then hurried around the back of the keep toward the kitchens. I blew out a breath, the heat that had been pummeling me for the past half hour gone and replaced with a cold as thick and frigid as ice.

Ever since I'd been brought back to the future, and I'd been able to hold Moira in my arms again, I knew it would be a crushing blow to be without her. I loved her deeply, more than I'd ever thought possible.

Och, and Logan had Emma with him for much longer. They'd just birthed a bairn. I couldn't imagine the pain he must be suffering at that moment.

Thick, dark clouds moved over the blue of the sky, pressing in on the sun. Dark and formidable. Was Fate taunting me?

I turned slowly back toward the main doors and walked with heavy steps toward the keep. Inside, the light barely hit the walls, obscured by the narrowness of the windows and the dark clouds.

I stood at the bottom of the circular stair, counting the steps until they rounded out of sight. I didn't want to go upstairs. I didn't want to tell my wife that Emma, her good friend, was gone. Missing. Vanished into thin air. That there was the possibility that she, Moira, one day could be gone, too, even though we both knew it was a possibility and happened to us both before. Hell, Moira was from a different time than modern day anyway. Hundreds of years in the past. And who knew what the time difference would be. Could be catastrophic.

ELIZA KNIGHT

When I'd gone to the future, only a couple days passed in my mind, but *years* passed in the Highlands. Five long years to be exact. Five years I'd lost and could never regain.

If time caught up with my wife, she'd long since have turned to dust. And me, too, for that matter, if I ended up in the future.

If my son, Ranulf, were ever to find out the fact that I'd time traveled, that I could disappear at any moment, along with my lady wife—a missing royal princess—his argument against me being chief of the MacLeod clan would be secured. Or else, the clan would think him mad. Or me. Who knew?

Either way, I couldn't risk it.

"Ballocks," I ground out and lifted my foot onto the first stair, but I couldn't make myself go any further.

I stood there, half suspended.

I ran a hand through my hair, feeling a cold sweat break out at my temples and along my spine. We were leaving within the hour. I had to go upstairs. Had to tell her what was happening. She needed to get dressed, to pack. I needed to pack. We needed provisions. There was much to be done, and I wasn't doing any of it just standing there.

"My laird?" Tomas, my steward, appeared from the darkness of the corridor, approaching with hesitation. His eyes shifted back and forth as he warily approached me. "Is ought amiss?"

I cleared my throat, shoving all the emotions tangled inside me somewhere else. "Lady Moira and I will be leaving within the hour with a dozen men."

"What's happened? Pardon my asking, my laird."

I waved away Tomas' manners. I'd yet to make any of the warriors a second in command, so while I was gone, Tomas was in charge.

"The Guardian has called me to service. I hope we will

not be gone long. The clan is to come to ye should they need anything."

"Ye're leaving me as acting laird?" Tomas raised a brow. No doubt, he thought it was odd that I'd yet to name a second, but he had to understand.

"Aye," I said with conviction.

Tomas nodded solemnly. "I will do my best in honoring your wishes, my laird. And what of Ranulf?"

I let out a deep sigh. "Can ye handle him? Keep him training? Or is it best for him to remain detained in his chamber? I dinna want the lad to cause trouble for ye. There will be enough of that."

I loathed the fact that I had to lock my own son up. But he was a danger to himself and others, Moira in particular. I'd seen the sneers he'd passed her way. Heard the threats he'd hissed about burning her at the stake. The lad had attempted to take my head more than once during training, not to mention when I'd had to challenge him in front of the clan at Gealach. I felt bad for him, too. He thought I'd dishonored his mother. He didn't know the truth. Poor lass. God rest her soul.

Though Ranulf hated me, I thought he might also resent that Moira had been my replacement for his mother in my mind. Perhaps when he'd learned that I'd loved Abi, he'd thought I sullied her name by loving another. Who knew? I'd contemplated the reasons behind his anger for so many hours, I could have watched the seasons turn.

"I can handle him," Tomas said.

"If ye find him to be unmanageable, ye have my permission to keep him in his chamber. Be sure that there are two guards with him at all times. He's been waiting for a moment to escape. With my absence, will likely come his courage to see it through."

"Aye, my laird. What else may I assist ye with in your absence?"

I could barely think. All I wanted to do was go upstairs and grasp Moira in my arms, but Tomas, and the entire clan, depended on me to keep it together. "The normal duties. Keep track of the plantings and harvest. Market day. Ledgers. Dispensing of coin if necessary. If need be judgments for the crofters, but if it can wait, please let it. If any messages come, and they are urgent, please forward them on to Gealach."

"Aye, my laird."

"As soon as I ascertain the situation at Castle Gealach, I will send word so ye have a better idea of when we will be returning. 'Tis my sincerest hope that we are returned within a fortnight, a month at most."

Tomas pressed his hand to his heart. "The clan and lands will be in good hands, ye have my word. I shall honor ye, my laird. Ye and our lady."

"I never doubted it." Tomas was the only man I'd learned to trust fully. There were a few guards, aye, but many more that I questioned their loyalty. Most of the men had known me previously, but of those men, at least half believed I'd abandoned the clan when I'd left after my uncle's death, years before. But they didn't understand. How could I have stayed when I feared his death was on my hands?

When I returned from this trip, I was going to have to put each and every one of them in their place. They needed to respect me as their laird or find another clan that would accept them. No longer could I walk around wondering who was loyal and who held a secret grudge. I was laird. I needed to act as such.

Tomas stared at me a moment longer, expecting something more. I'd been putting off going upstairs and now it was obvious I was putting off dismissing him, too.

Mo chreach. I needed to go to Moira. Needed to tell her

what happened. Already a good quarter hour had passed. We had even less time to get ready to depart now.

"That is all, Tomas. If ye would see a bag of provisions packed for us and the men?"

"Aye, my laird."

I didn't wait for Tomas to leave, I turned my back on him and took the stairs three at a time, reaching the level that housed our bedchamber. The door was locked and I pulled the key from around my neck to unlock it.

Moira lay on the bed, a mischievous grin on her delicious lips as she sat up to take me in.

"You weren't able to last very long," she teased, but then, taking note of my grim look, she sat straight up, her face paling. "What's happened?"

Rather than beat around the bush like I wanted to, I simply came out with it. "Emma is missing. The messenger says it's as though she vanished. No clue as to who could have taken her."

"Missing... Vanished." Moira frowned, but her mind connected the meaning behind those words a lot faster than mine had. Her gaze jolted upward to meet mine, and her visage paled another shade. "Oh, no..."

"Aye. We must go. Logan has requested our presence."

She leaned forward to untie the cords at her ankles and I rushed to help her.

"I can't believe this," she murmured. "What about Shona? How is my sister? Is she still there?"

"There was no mention of Shona or her husband. Only Emma. But I should think if something happened to them, there would have been news in regards to that as well."

Moira leapt from the bed and rushed to the wardrobe, tugging out a clean chemise and plaid gown. She looked good dressed in the costume of my time, though I sure did miss the tight pants she'd worn in the modern era.

"Logan must be devastated," she said. "And poor Saor must be desperate for his mother."

"Aye." I couldn't form any other words. I could only imagine what their pain was like, and it ripped at my insides.

Moira whipped around and ran toward me, throwing herself in my arms. She buried her face in the crook of my shoulder, wetness warming my skin. She was crying.

"I hope this doesn't mean..." But she trailed off, not voicing the fear we both had.

"Ye're still here," I said. "I'm still here. We will make the most of every precious minute. Let this just be a reminder to us that we are not in control of our place in time. That we must cherish each other always."

Moira nodded, shuddering. "I'm scared."

"Me, too." I rarely admitted fear. I was a man, a warrior, but this was the one thing that had always terrified me.

We held each other a few more minutes, both of us wound tight, and then quietly we parted, each of us packing a satchel in silence. Stealing long glances. We walked quietly, hand in hand, down the corridor, the stairs, and then out the front doors.

Our horses awaited us along with twelve grim-faced warriors and two pack mules and servants.

"We'll not need the servants," I said to Tomas.

He frowned, and rather than argue with him, I said, "Never mind."

I walked Moira to her horse, but when I moved to assist her, she squeezed me tight and whispered, "Can I ride with you for a little while? Not for long, I promise. I just need to be close to you."

I didn't hesitate. "Aye, love."

We mounted my horse and I nodded to Tomas.

"Where are ye going?" The shriek was far off, and shrill.

I glanced up at the tower to see Ranulf's angry face

peering from his window. I'd forgotten to tell him that I was leaving. There was no time now. Another thing the lad was going to hold against me.

I raised my hand in a salute, but he didn't return my gesture. I wasn't surprised, but his disapproval wasn't something I could worry about now.

Maybe he wouldn't have to worry over it either, for there was every chance I wouldn't return.

❧ 9 ❧

EMMA

The wine pouring red and slick reminded me of blood oozing from a wound. Perhaps the wound carved in my heart.

"I don't know what you're talking about," I said to Mr. McAlister in regards to his comment about me knowing where Moira was.

That wasn't *exactly* a lie. I didn't know at this very moment where Moira or Shona were, I only knew the era, and even that was questionable given my own current situation.

The man who called himself a solicitor didn't say anything, but continued to pour three glasses of wine. He held one out first to Mrs. MacDonald and then one to me.

I hesitated and his brows rose.

"Take it," he said. Not a bit of consternation or threat in his tone. "The vintage is divine."

I took the glass, trying to keep my hand steady. I swirled the wine in the cup, sniffed. It smelled good. Oaky and fruity undertones. Judging from the scent, it would be good. And I was struck then with such a sense of ridiculousness. I'd just been forced five hundred years in the future, leaving behind my husband, my newborn, all of my friends, and I was sniffing wine.

Mr. McAlister raised his glass in the air and said, "To new beginnings."

But, I refused to cheer to that. I didn't want a new beginning. I wanted my old life back. However, I couldn't very well say that aloud, so instead, I raised my glass and thought: *To finding Logan. Reuniting with Saor.*

The wine swished over my tongue, as delicious as its fragrance. As divine as McAlister had said it was.

"Your stew smells mighty fine," McAlister said to Mrs. MacDonald.

My stomach grumbled, evidently also believing it smelled good, though my mouth was dry. I took another sip of wine, surprised at how very good it really was, hoping that by wetting my tongue, I'd also whet my appetite. I needed to eat. To keep up my strength. It wouldn't do to search for a way back if I had not the energy to stand.

"Oh, yes, let us eat." Mrs. MacDonald set down her glass and rushed back to the stove.

She dished out three generous portions into bowls and I set out spoons, knives and forks on top of napkins at the very table Moira and Rory had been sitting at a couple weeks ago —if Mr. McAlister's estimation of when Moira disappeared could be believed.

I flattened my hand on the surface, smoothing my palm over the wood, hoping to draw comfort from something a friend had touched.

My heart ached; a permanent lump resided in my throat. I swallowed around it, telling myself to remain strong through this meal; else, these two know the exact depth of my despair, leaving me at quite the disadvantage.

We ate mostly in silence, thank goodness. The stew was

fragrant, but tasteless on my tongue. I was simply too numb to enjoy it. Even the wine had lost its luster.

When Mrs. MacDonald was clearing the table, the solicitor pulled out a picture and placed it on the surface, sliding it toward me.

"Recognize that?" he asked.

I gazed down at the snapshot, my friends' faces smiling back at me. Shona with her fiery red locks and Moira with dark, unruly curls. They were dressed stylishly, and the background looked to be that of a flower storeroom. Probably their herbal shop. Puzzling though, was why he'd ask if I recognized *that*... "You mean, them, not that?"

"Nay."

What the heck was he talking about? I stared at his wine glass, certain he must have had too much to drink.

"What do ye see around Moira's neck?" he urged.

I stared at the same necklace I'd seen her wear at Gealach, the one we'd found out had been given to her by her true parents—the king and queen of Scotland, who'd lived almost two hundred years before 1544.

Did McAlister know what he was asking? What he was looking at?

"The necklace?" I managed to keep my voice from wavering.

"And ye recognize it do ye not?" He nodded, as if trying to prompt me to answer his way.

I met his gaze, seeing the intensity. I shrugged. "I don't know," I lied.

He leaned forward in his chair, flicking his eyes back to Mrs. MacDonald who'd turned on the sink and was humming as she soaped up the dinner dishes.

"Look, the two of us are going to have to work together," he said.

"Or what?" Lord, what was happening? My head swam from exhaustion, fear, anxiety, wine.

"Finding Moira."

I shook my head. "I'm looking for someone else."

Oh, why had I admitted that? I guess I just wanted the man to leave me alone.

"Who?"

"Nobody," I whispered, feeling guilty for having said that. Logan and Saor were everything me.

"I know ye've no reason to trust me. Less reason to trust me than the woman who is helping ye, I get that. But *I* need your help. Moira could be in grave danger."

"Moira?" I knew she was in grave danger if she ended up in the wrong time, but she was nearly two hundred years in the future from the time when she was an heiress to the throne. And yes, there had been some fear when Rory's son had brought the MacDonald to Gealach, and the man had nearly put two and two together, but with Rory and Moira making up a new identity and the necklace safely locked away, Moira was safe. And Shona, no one knew who she was. Her already established position as the Lady of the Wood kept her secure.

"Aye." He sat back, looking with irritation in the direction of Mrs. MacDonald who was still washing dishes. I got the feeling he wanted her to disappear. "Have ye heard of the time jumpers?" he whispered.

I'd had to crane my neck to hear what he said; I wasn't so sure I'd actually wanted to hear that. Time jumpers? I pressed my lips together and shook my head, dismissing him. "Sounds like a science fiction novel."

He frowned at me and leaned forward again. "Let us both not pretend that I dinna know where ye came from, lassie. We both know ye're not from around here."

"I've made no pretense of hiding where I'm from. Even

Mrs. MacDonald knows. I'm from the U.S., Washington, D.C.," I said, still denying what I knew he knew.

"Right." He rolled his eyes toward the ceiling and took a long swallow from his wine. "Let's just say, for fun, that ye may have once been from the States, but now ye're from somewhere else."

"I came here today from Drumnadrochit." I pushed the picture back across the table. "She drove me, you can ask her."

Mr. McAlister visibly gritted his teeth. "What year is Moira in?"

Wow. I hadn't expected him to just come right out with that. And I supposed I was getting nowhere denying it. He didn't believe me and even though I didn't trust him, maybe I could confide in him, as long as I tread lightly, because just maybe, he knew how I could get back there.

I waited a moment, letting the air between us fill with tension. By the sink, Mrs. MacDonald was still humming, though I could see she was working on the pot. Not long until she was completely done. I blew out a breath and blurted, "1544."

McAlister sat back in his chair and let out a long, weary filled sigh. He crossed his arms over his chest, shaking his head. "This is not good."

"Why?" I asked.

"As I mentioned, there are time jumpers." He looked exasperated that I didn't seem to understand what the hell time jumpers were. "Ye've not heard of them, seriously?"

I shook my head, bristling. "Honestly."

"They are the keeper of secrets. A society of sorts, with the ability to time travel whenever they please. They hold a dear secret of our mutual friends."

This was too much; I just wanted to go home. "Behind the Ayreshire lassies' birth?"

"Ye know of it?" he murmured, his gaze once more flicking to Mrs. MacDonald.

She hummed as she wiped the dishes dry, clinking them as she put them back in the cabinets.

I nodded, and murmured the poem I'd heard months before. "One of red and one of black, born at Ayreshire and swept back, lost forever the princesses of time, the last of the king's most sacred line."

Moira and Shona were the Ayreshire lassies. The firstborn —Moira—was given a pendant that belonged to her mother, a golden circle to represent the crown with a lion etched on top of it to show the joined houses of Scotland and England. Their blood could have united the countries, but their mother feared for their lives. Legend stated that their father was a prisoner of the English King Edward III. If Edward had known King David had children, he would have killed Moira and Shona to keep his crown.

"Aye." Mr. McAlister let out a breath I'd not realized he was holding.

"But..." I shook my head and swallowed down the last dregs of wine in my glass. "They don't know anything."

"Everyone thought it was safer that way."

"Who is everyone?"

"Their mother. Me."

Their mother... I still remembered to this day how devastated they'd looked when they found out who they were and that they'd never get a chance to meet their parents. "Who are you?"

He glanced at Mrs. MacDonald and then back at me. "I think it best we talk later."

"Why?"

He moved his eyes back and forth, indicating the woman who'd helped me. I glanced at her and Mrs. MacDonald smiled, wiping her hands dry on a towel.

"Is everything all right?" she asked. "How about some dessert? I saw a pie in the fridge."

"Apple," Mr. McAlister said. "Moira's favorite."

I nodded, forcing a bright smile to my face, because I didn't want Mrs. MacDonald to think anything strange was happening, but my mind was a jumble of confusion.

Mr. McAlister didn't trust Mrs. MacDonald.

I didn't completely trust either of them.

And I'd opened up and told McAlister things that were sacred. Secrets that if they got into the wrong hands could be damaging to my loved ones and me. And yet, it was a risk I'd had to take on the off chance he could help me.

The pie was served, and though it was delicious, I could barely eat more than two bites. I stood up from the table, carrying my plate to the sink. "I'm exhausted. If you'll excuse me. Mrs. MacDonald, thank you so much for dinner, and Mr. McAlister, it was great to meet you."

"I'll be in touch," Mr. McAlister said.

"There's no need, really. I won't be here long."

"Sweet dreams, dear." Mrs. MacDonald's gaze shifted over me oddly, made me feel uncomfortable for a moment, as though she wished me the exact opposite in truth. A night filled with nightmares, which in all likelihood, unless I met Logan again upon the glen, a sleep filled with terror seemed very likely.

Her sinister glance was fleeting and I wondered if I'd just imagined it. Her eyes sparkled at me and she smiled sweetly.

"Good night," I murmured, without energy to examine her strange behavior further.

I wandered up the stairs, a stranger in a house full of strangers. Inside Shona's room, I locked the door. Definitely more conscious than automatic. I felt safer behind a lock.

A few moments later, I heard the front door open and close. I slipped from bed to peek between the blinds. Mr.

McAlister stood in the dim shine of the lamppost. He was staring at Mrs. MacDonald's car and then back at the house. He slipped something from his pocket, walked around the back of the car and keeping his eye on the house, ducked behind the trunk.

A moment later, he rose and jogged across the street, waiting a few moments in the shadows before climbing into another vehicle, which must have been his own.

What had he been doing to her car? What was the thing in his hand? A tracking device? That went way beyond simply not trusting someone to all out freaky stalking.

Definitely fishy. My earlier thoughts about him not trusting the woman downstairs were confirmed and then some.

Though he'd gotten into his car, he didn't pull away. He didn't even turn it on. Like he was hiding. Or waiting.

What was he waiting for?

I wanted to wrench open the window and shout that very question. What the heck was going on? What was all the mystery? Why did I feel so lost in a world that should be more familiar to me than the one I lived in?

1544 was a brutal time, yes, but it was also so simple.

Downstairs I could hear Mrs. MacDonald shuffling around. The sound of voices had my spine stiffening, my pulse skyrocketing. But it was only the television. An old re-run of *Friends*, it sounded like.

For goodness' sake, Mr. McAlister had me all sorts of freaked out.

No longer as exhausted as I had been after dinner, too intrigued with the mystery, I sat in the window box, tucking my knees up toward my chest, wincing at the ache in my breasts, and waited. I wasn't sure what it was I was waiting for, but that didn't matter. I was too freaked out to sleep. My imagination was running wild with the legend of the

Ayreshire girls and talk of time jumpers. And spies. And bad guys.

If I even tried to sleep, that was all I was likely to dream about. I shivered, rubbing at the goosebumps on my arms.

I just wanted to go home. To have Saor in my arms, as Logan cradled me in his.

I squinted out the window, trying to be non-conspicuous behind the blinds, as if that was going to help me see better into Mr. McAlister's car. Was he going to sleep there? Did he think something was going to happen?

Was something going to happen?

Every time someone walked down the street, I nearly leapt out of my skin. When the nosy neighbor lady came out of her house to put a bag of trash at the roadside, I held my breath, half expecting men clad in black suits to leap from nowhere and grab her.

But what I didn't expect was the front door to open and Mrs. MacDonald to step outside. I squeezed myself against the wall, straightened out my legs, trying to become one with the house around me as I watched her.

She crept down the few stairs and onto the walkway, looking back and forth. When she glanced up at the house, I ducked further down, even though I knew she couldn't see me. The blinds were turned in a way she couldn't, no light was on in the room to show my shadow.

She headed toward her car and opened the passenger door, leaning in and riffling around. When she came out, she held a black box in her hand, maybe the size of a block of cheese. I couldn't make out more than its shape and color. It could have been anything. Something mundane and boring, or something as wacky and spy-like as the tracker I was certain McAlister had put under her car.

With another glance around, Mrs. MacDonald ran back inside, the door closing with a near inaudible click beneath me. She didn't want me to know she'd left. That was clear by the way she tiptoed around, and from the blaring of the television.

As soon as she was inside, McAlister climbed from his car and ran back across the street toward the house. He ducked into an alleyway around the side and out of view.

Dammit! Where was he going?

I tried to imagine what the backyard had looked like when I was out there. Was there a gate in their fence? An alleyway along the side? I couldn't remember.

Downstairs the television kicked up a notch, but a creak on the stairs had every single hair on my body standing on end.

Had my savior from Steven turned up the television to mask the sound of her approach?

Oh shit...

Just who was Mrs. MacDonald? Did a name leap centuries? Was she my enemy? Was she one of those, time jumpers that McAlister had warned me about?

As quietly as I could, I climbed down from the window box seat and looked around the room, searching for something, anything, I could use as a weapon.

My eyes lit on a tennis racket in the corner.

Another creak, this time from outside of my room. I crept to the corner, picking up the racket. It was light, but hopefully a good swing would be all I needed to get around the old bat.

The door handle jiggled, the distinct sound rattling louder in my pounding head.

Was she going to kill me? Try to abduct me?

"Mrs. MacDonald?" Speak of the devil... McAlister's voice floated back up the stairs.

There was a thump on the outside of my door and then the scuffle of footsteps. Groans and grunts.

"What are ye doing here?" Her voice was muffled, angry and further away as though she'd moved back to the top of the stairs.

I couldn't hear McAlister's reply, but seconds later there was a loud thumping sound coming from the stairs, muffled curses.

They might just kill each other.

If I'd not been scared out of my damned mind, I might have thought the idea of a fight between two elderly people to be a thing of comedy.

But I was scared, frightened for my life.

I stared at the box window. Perhaps it would be the second window I'd climbed out of today.

❦ 10 ❦

LOGAN

Three misery filled days had passed since I'd sent a summons to Rory and Moira.

Every night I'd spent in the glen. As soon as gloaming descended upon the Highlands, I rowed across the loch and marched up the mountainside, bursting into the stone circle as though a dragon waited there for me to slay.

And every time I whirled in a circle wanting to see Emma, or to face off with Fate, I found myself, utterly and undeniably alone.

I had long conversations with the charged air around me. Why had Fate forsaken me? What could I do to prove myself, to bring Emma back?

But the only answer I received was the same mocking silence

I'd fall asleep, staring up at the star-filled sky. Or the cloud covered sky, and I'd endure the rain as it fell upon my head.

I waited for Emma to fill my dreams, but every morning I woke having not seen her, a fact that made me extremely fearful for her safety.

Shona had been hard at work pouring over books in the

library and fleshing out old wives tales that might have had anything even the least bit to deal with magic.

Nothing had yet worked.

Not even a sign.

Nor a glimmer of hope.

Even Saor seemed to notice that his mama was gone. The bairn had grown quiet, his cries not as forceful. The nurse-maid said he was eating well and sleeping, but the fact that he'd grown so quiet worried me. He stared vigilantly at the world around him, as if hoping he might just catch the sound of his mother on the wind.

I paced the courtyard, still wet from my swim. I rarely went inside. Each morning when I trudged dejectedly back down the mountain, I dove into the loch, plunging deep and searching the bottom, just in case it wasn't Fate that had taken her.

Emma would never have taken her own life, but that didn't mean one of my enemies wouldn't.

Thank the saints I came up empty-handed each time.

I studied the sky, searching out even the smallest hint of a breeze that might show me she was coming back, or that Fate had something more in store for us.

"My laird, can I bring ye something to break your fast?"

I looked at the servant who approached, possibly the one to have drawn the shortest straw. A different one came to me at each meal during the day. Their eyes were also shifty, their steps too close together, bodies taught as if prepared to run.

I grunted. "Whisky."

I found a dram of whisky every morning helped to settle the fears charging through my brain enough to get my mind thinking. I'd have liked to barricade myself on the battle-ments where I could see far and wide with a barrel of whisky to numb the pain. But being inebriated wasn't going to help me find my wife, and likely it would make me feel worse than I already did.

The servant nodded and hurried away. I continued my pacing, glaring up at the clear blue sky. When Emma had been brought to my time the sun had not been shining. A massive storm she'd said had been taking place—but that was on her end of the timeline. My end had been a decent Highland day. Much like this one.

"Good morning," Shona murmured.

I'd not heard her approach. She held out a cup of whisky and a bannock cake. Guess the servant had passed off the task to someone less likely to get their head chewed off.

"Breakfast," she said.

I nodded, swigging down the whisky and biting into the cake.

"Am I really so terrifying?" I asked.

Shona laughed, the joyful sounded twinged with loss. "Nay. Not to me." She cleared her throat, standing beside me both of us looking toward the gate. "Will Moira be arriving today?" she asked, an edge to her voice.

I got the sense she'd been working her way to asking me. Perhaps, I was terrifying. "I pray 'tis so." I tried to say it softly, to put her and myself at ease. But it didn't work. The tension inside me only seemed to grow.

"I have an idea, and I'm not sure you're going to be open to it," she said, crossing and then uncrossing her arms.

"I'll be the judge of that. Tell me."

Shona fiddled with her belt. Tightening it even though it was already tight. "The glen has magical powers, especially when one is giving themselves over to... passion."

I'd told her about the dream, about seeing Emma and that it was real. That it wasn't the first time our spirits had made love. Shona hadn't flinched. Emma had told her about the magical powers of the glen, and she'd taken Ewan up to the top. That was how they'd been able to conceive a child when all else seemed to have failed.

"I've gone to the glen every night since the first one," I said. "But I've not seen her again."

"I'm thinking, that if all five of us are there. Me and Ewan, Moira and Rory, ye, that we might be able to make a bigger, more powerful impact on the glen's magic."

What she said, hinted at, suddenly dawned on me. "Ye're talking about a massive... Saints, what's the word...?"

Shona's face flamed red and she nearly choked when she uttered, "Orgy."

"Ah, aye, an orgy." I'd participated in many and I knew Ewan was fond of them also. But that was before we'd both fallen in love.

"Yes, well, I think that we should try it," she hurried on. "None of the other things I've been trying have been working. Nor, pardon my saying so, have your attempts."

"Does that mean I'll be...?" I pointed between her and myself. "And with Ewan and Rory..."

"Oh!" Shona's face glowed even redder than it already was, if that was possible. "No, no, no. We'd all be making love to each other, but separately." She frowned. "Me with Ewan. Rory with Moira, and you, summoning Emma."

"Good." That could cause a host of issues. I found Moira and Shona attractive, but not in a way other than a genuine observance. Emma was the only woman for me. Besides, if we were all to participate in something like that, it would likely put an awkward wedge in our tight bond.

"And what if we all end up in modern day?" I asked, terrified of the unknown, the loudness. All the contraptions and rules I didn't understand.

"If you're with Emma would it matter?" Shona asked, turning to look me in the eye for the first time since handing me my breakfast.

I nodded. "Aye... My son..."

Shona's eyes went downcast. "There is a chance that we will all end up time traveling and not simply bringing Emma back. But I strongly believe that we were all meant to be in this time. Why else would we all be here? Think about it, me, Moira, Emma, Ewan, we aren't from this time. We're not even all from the *same* time. If we ended up in the modern era, Fate will see us brought back."

"I'm not sure that's something I can risk. Not with a son left behind who needs protection. Ye recall how many want my head? They will leap at the chance to see my son buried in my absence."

"Hide him away while we go up to the glen. Tell whoever it is watching him that if ye dinna return that they are to claim him as their own, to find another clan and to never ever say who Saor really is."

The thought of losing my son tore at my gut. How could I even contemplate the possibility? And then there was Emma... She would murder me if she knew I even thought about it.

But life without Emma... It wasn't worth living for me, and if there was a chance I could bring her back, to save her from whatever Fate had tossed at her, then I wanted to. I'd just have to pray my son was safe. Ballocks, but this was a hard decision.

"I will do it," I ground out.

Shona bit her lip. "I pray the others agree. The moon will be full tonight giving us the highest chances for the magic to work."

"And that makes a difference..." I'd heard mention of it before. "It wasn't full the night she disappeared."

"Sometimes, people simply disappear for no reason other than Fate has taken a chance." She hurried to add. "I know it isn't fair, Logan. I know it doesn't make sense."

I nodded solemnly. "And we need to take a chance then to get her back. Fate wants to see us chance as much as she has."

"Maybe Fate is testing you. To see how deep your love goes. Emma or Saor."

"That is not a choice I'm willing to make."

"Theoretically, no, but perhaps in this instance, yes?"

"I will go to the glen. To see if the magic can bring Emma back to us, but I do not want to leave my son."

Shona let out a deep sigh. I could tell she was frustrated with me, with my line of thought. I was frustrated that I even had to contemplate it.

But there did not appear to be any other way. Through gritted teeth, I laid out the plan that she'd suggested. "I will see that he and his nursemaid are tucked away with a guard, that if I should not come back, they are to leave Grant lands under the guise they are a family."

"We will find her, and the three of you will be reunited." Her words, spoken in a stronger tone, would have left me with hope, but they weren't strong, they were laced with doubt, the same doubt that assaulted me every minute of every day for the past three days.

The guards on the battlements shouted a warning, and voices could be heard from the other side. For a split second hope soared that it was Emma, returned from wherever she'd been. But then I heard our friends call out from the other side of the wall.

"Rory and Moira are here," I said.

The gates were opened; the portcullis raised and in rode the two of them with a dozen guards at their backs.

Rory dismounted, helping his wife down, who ran to her twin sister.

I approached Rory, holding out my arm and he shook it. Then I pulled Moira to me, kissing her cheek.

"We're here to help," she said.

"My thanks," I replied. "Shona has a theory that she thinks could work."

Ewan jogged down the gate tower stairs and approached us. He clapped Rory on the back and embraced Moira.

"Did she tell ye?" Ewan eyed me warily.

I nodded. "We will go tonight."

"Where?" Rory asked.

"Shona believes that if all of us go to the glen on a night like tonight, where there is a full moon, and we engage in passionate acts, that the power of it will break open whatever capsule of magic is needed to bring Emma back," I explained.

"Passionate acts?" Rory raised a brow.

"These acts of passion..." Ewan said, glancing at me. "Did she explain that we'd be...?" Ewan cleared his throat.

Shona gasped. "I did. It's not going to be *that* type of orgy..."

Rory looked confused. "What type?"

Moira leaned up and whispered in his ear. His eyes widened.

Shona giggled, then elbowed Ewan. "'Haps I should call upon Hildie and a few of her lassies to come help, eh, Ewan?"

I grunted a laugh. Ewan had often engaged in passionate acts with more than one woman at a time before he'd met Shona.

Ewan stroked a hand over Shona's belly. "'Haps a night of lovemaking will entice our young bairn to join the world."

Watching the two loving couples made my heart seize. I couldn't take it.

Rory cut into the affectionate display. "There is the possibility we will end up in the future."

"I know it," I said through gritted teeth. "Though I'm not happy over it. I just want her back. Go and settle in. I need some air. I'll meet ye at the gates tonight."

They eyed me oddly, for I was already outside, but I

ignored them, charging off through the gates, reckless and uncaring that my enemies often waited for such a chance.

☙❦☙

THE MOON ROSE UP IN THE SKY. A GIANT SILVER GLOBE with a yellow hallo. Stars dotted the inky blackness, winking, taunting me with the magic they held but had not released for me.

All five of us stood in the center of the clearing, awkwardly smiling and looking nervous. A few attempts were made at mindless comments but then someone would forget to speak and silence reigned again.

My gut wrenched.

We were about to embark on something truly mad. A moment in our relationship that I'm certain none of us had thought to ever encounter, and yet, if we did and it worked, we could very well bring Emma home. And if it didn't... Well, then we'd always have these awkward moments to remember.

"Let's stand in a circle round the center stone," Shona said. "We'll hold hands and tell Fate exactly what we want."

We moved to do as she suggested, our feet barely making a sound in the soft grass. Shona was to my left, Ewan to my right, Moira and Rory in front of me—though their faces were blocked by the thickness of the stone we surrounded. Ewan's grip was steady, strong; Shona's was firm but shaky.

Mine was somewhere in between.

I stared hard at the sacred stone, willing it to light up as it had done in my dream. It remained coldly stark.

"Fate!" Shona shouted, her face toward the sky.

They all looked toward the sky with her, but I stared firmly at the stone, willing it to know what I wanted. Willing it to light with magic.

"Bring us our Emma back. Bring Emma Gordon Grant

back to this time. Back to her husband, Logan, her child, Saor, and her friends. We beg of you!"

She repeated the words again, and we all followed, saying the words with her, louder and louder still, until it was more a chant than a prayer. Our hands all steadied, strong and forceful as we gripped each other.

Rays of moonlight touched the stone in streaks, reminding me of sword blades. They stabbed down from the sky, cutting into the natural world.

Did the moon know my pain? Did Fate?

"Bring her back to me!" I bellowed.

"And now..." Shona murmured, letting go of my hand. She kept her gaze only on Ewan as she walked toward him and put her arms around his neck. They leaned toward each other, bodies connecting at the same time as their lips.

The intimate move was well practiced. Sensual.

I was envious, my gut twisting with jealousy. I wanted Emma. To wrap my arms around her and show her how much I loved her with a sweet kiss.

Moira and Rory followed suit. Their kiss was filled with such passion. The spark of excitement that newlyweds often felt. Hungry. Craving. All consuming.

I turned away from them, heading to the other side of the glen. I lay on the ground, hands behind my head and stared up at the moon.

How many times had I watched it, waiting for something to happen? This would be the fourth night I'd laid here. I prayed it wasn't as disappointing as the last three. I wanted to see her. To hold her, even if it was only her spirit.

Across the way, four moans rose up to join in the soft wails of a breeze. I could hear the sounds of them kissing, stroking, connecting. None of them were taking this chore lightly, putting passion to the test.

Tingles coursed through my body, my veins. And it wasn't

from being turned on. This was different. A charge of fire that whizzed through my veins. I'd not felt like this before. Not even the night I'd dreamed of Emma.

I closed my eyes, wondering if sleep was calling. If the magic of the glen would bring her to me.

But my eyes refused to close other than a few precious blinks. They stared wide open at the sky, hopeful and fearful at the same time. Was my mind fighting it? My fear of being taken from Saor?

I glanced at the stone, seeing the moon's blades slicing against it. But no other light.

"What do I do?" I whispered. "Emma…"

The tingles increased, flowing hot and cold through my veins, expanding, until they reached my neck with a painful force. I felt my veins pulsing hard, my heart seizing. My back arched of its own volition, gut wrenching toward the sky. My vision blurred. My mouth went dry. A silent scream on my lips.

And then, the moon's glow disappeared.

11

EMMA

The front door opened and closed, followed by silence. I stood still for only a moment before rushing to the window to see who had left, but the streets were clear.

I wasn't crazy. I knew I'd heard the door open and close.

Now definitely wasn't the time to start thinking I was losing my mind. I mean, I'd traveled back in time, then forward, married another man and had a baby. If I was going to start questioning my mental health because of a front door, there were bigger problems I wasn't considering.

I stared hard out the window. Not a single soul in sight.

But, oddly, both their cars were gone. Had it taken me longer than I thought to get to the window? Had I just missed them? Were they speed demons as well as boxers? I certainly believed Mrs. MacDonald could race like that.

"Ohmygod," I whispered to myself, backing away from the window.

On second thought, maybe I was crazy.

Or maybe, as real as this felt, it wasn't. I was having a

nightmare or a breakdown or something. I was stuck in some sort of hell, that was for certain.

This was supposed to be my safe house. The first place I'd thought of at Mrs. Lamb's to get away from the chaos, from Steven. But it had become quite the opposite now. An *unsafe* house.

Then again, this house actually proved I wasn't crazy. Moira and Shona were real people, and I knew them.

I stood stock still for maybe five whole minutes. Listening. Waiting. Just in case Mrs. MacDonald or McAlister came back, or never left and the closing of the door had been a trick of my mind.

I didn't know who either of them was, but I did know I couldn't trust them. That was abundantly clear.

When no sounds came other than the occasional car whizzing past on the street below, I grabbed my purse and slung it crisscross over my shoulders and chest.

I needed to leave.

I didn't know where I'd go, or how I'd get there, but I wasn't staying here another minute.

Holding the tennis racket, just in case, I unlocked and opened the door, blinking into the darkness of the upstairs hallway when a shadow loomed in front.

"Hello, dear," Steven said, his voice low and menacing.

Ohmygod...

I backed away from the door in complete shock and disbelieve. The tennis racket fell from my numb fingers. Bile rose up my throat.

"What... What are you doing here?" I asked, jerking my head toward the window. "How did you get here?"

He followed me into the room, blocking the door from my view. "Now, that's no way to treat your husband is it?"

I shook my head, my foot getting caught on the racket, nearly toppling me backward.

He laughed as I righted myself.

"You're not my husband," I said, sternly. More stern than I'd ever spoken to him before.

"Tsk, tsk." He looked behind him, and I did too, not sure what to expect. "I see you met my friend."

"Friend?" That had to explain how he'd found me. But which one was his friend?

"Mrs. MacDonald. Though I'm surprised you followed her, given the name."

"What...?" My breath caught. Steven... *knew?*

No, no, no. I shook my head, trying to clear away the chaos, but it only buzzed louder in my ears.

He waved his hand and rolled his eyes. "Oh, I know, right about now you're questioning all sorts of things aren't you? Well, let me clear it up real quick for you." He cleared his throat and crossed his arms over his chest, staring down at me as though I were easily the biggest moron he'd ever laid eyes on. "When you disappeared, Mrs. MacDonald was in and out of Mrs. Lamb's house. She caught my attention. Turns out, the woman is a time jumper, but I suspect you know what that is so I won't go into detail. Long story short, she and I formed a friendship, and she told me where you were. What you were doing. Or should I say, *who* you were doing." He sneered. "She told me it would only be a matter of time before you returned and when you came back, she promised to keep an eye on you. For me. Until I could get you all to myself. Didn't want to have Mrs. Lamb meddling again."

I swallowed hard around the lump in my throat.

"Suffice it to say, I'm not letting you out of my sight." He made a tsking sound. "Been there, done that."

I cleared my throat. "Where did they go?" I asked, nodding toward the hallway.

"Oh, them?" He hooked his thumb over his shoulder. "Well, they left. Probably won't ever see them again."

"But where?"

Steven narrowed his eyes. "Why do you care? They aren't going to help you. No one is."

I stiffened. "I *don't* care." But I did. Had they jumped back in time, changed history somehow and that's why their cars weren't there anymore, or had they simply driven away when he arrived?

If they could change history, anyone could. Even Steven. He could take me back in time to before I ever left for Gealach in the first place, making Logan and Saor and all my friends disappear. I shuddered.

Steven reached out with lightning speed and grabbed my wrist, yanking me toward him.

"You, sweet wife"—though when he said sweet it had more of a *bitch* tone to it—"Aren't going anywhere."

Steven tossed me down on the bed, and I bounced wildly, trying to scramble to the other side before he was one top of me.

"No!" I shouted. I wasn't going to let him touch me. Not like I'd let him so many times when we were married. He might be able to have me sinking back inside myself, quivering in fear, but the fact of the matter was, I was a changed a woman. I was stronger. More confident. More knowledgeable. I kicked and punched beneath him, tried to scratch his face, but he caught my wrists and slammed them up over my head, sending a shooting pain through my shoulders.

"Just what the hell do you think you're doing? You're my wife and this is my right."

I leaned up, looking him dead in the eye. "I. Am. Not. *Your.* Wife," I said through gritted teeth. "You mean nothing to me. And I do not belong to you."

He only laughed and squeezed my arms harder. I would have bruises tomorrow, I was certain. As long as there was a tomorrow...

"You'll do your wifely duties, whether you want to or not."

Wifely duties... He meant lay there while he raped me.

The room around me vibrated. I wasn't getting enough oxygen with him lying on top of me. I wasn't the waif I was when married to him before, but he was still bigger and his weight was crushing.

The air seemed to shift, the walls closing in.

"What the—?" Steven said, jerking backward.

He still kept me pinned as he scanned the oddly pulsing room.

So, it wasn't me. He saw it, too.

"Oh, thank God," I murmured. It was the time warp, had to be. I was leaving, or least I prayed I was leaving. I remembered this odd shift in the air from when I'd first time traveled, though I remembered nothing from the second time. Only waking up at Mrs. Lamb's.

Steven stared hard at me, trying to figure out what it was I was saying as the room around us began to vibrate in earnest, like an earthquake.

I just closed my eyes and waited for it to be over. Waited to find myself lying in a pasture or my own bed at Gealach.

But a second later, the room stopped shaking, and Steven's weight was still on top of me. The darkness of the room caving in around me, making it hard to breathe.

I opened my eyes to find his menacing glare.

"What were you saying?" he asked.

My tongue felt thick, my lungs tight, heart pounded.

Nothing had happened. I looked around the room, trying not to do so frantically, but I couldn't help it. Everything was the same.

Was it an earthquake? No! I couldn't believe that it would be. This couldn't be all there was, the half-broken promises of Fate. Fate was supposed to be good and kind and give people what they deserved. I didn't deserve this. I knew that.

"Get off me," I seethed. "Get *the fuck* off me. Now."

But Steven only laughed at my words, not giving a crap about my anger, my hatred. I bucked and kicked and yanked at his hold on my arms.

I had to be my own hero. Save myself from him. I couldn't wait for Fate to intervene. I needed to get away from this man, right now.

"I'm not letting you go. Ever."

"You don't have a choice. You don't own me."

He sneered. "Then maybe my new friend can send us to a time where I do."

I shook my head, that idea never having occurred to me.

"She's gone," I hissed.

"Not for long."

Was that the vibrations then? Mrs. MacDonald trying to jump back through time?

The feelings of helplessness I'd so often felt in our marriage returned. Of being oppressed, suffocated, left with no control over anything in my own life.

"Say it, Emma, say what you're really thinking." Steven's eyes were wide, maniacal.

"You don't want to hear what I have to say." This time it was me who sneered with disgust.

"Oh, but I do." His voice had taken on a jovial note. The kind he used when he was truly pissed.

Well, I was pissed, too. And I was ready to let him have it. "I hate you. I loathe the very ground you walk on, the air you breathe. I'd rather die than spend another minute with you in this lifetime or any other."

My outburst only made him laugh. His head reared back, mouth agape and the sound that issued was what I imagined a possessed donkey howling was like. The laughing stopped just as abruptly as it had started.

"I won't let that happen, my love. I want you nice and

warm." He bent low, trying to kiss me, but I bit his lip, drawing blood.

The metallic taste of it rolled over my tongue and I gagged.

He let go of my arms, but only so he could wrench back and slap me hard on the cheek.

The pain was instant—face throbbing, vision blurred.

Even still, if he tried to kiss me again, I'd bite him once more. Harder, and I wouldn't let go, like a savage beast, I'd tear at his flesh.

"You vicious little bitch. Is this what you learned while you were away? While you were off fucking some barbarian? I'm going to teach you a lesson in respect. I dare you to ever make a move against me again."

Steven climbed off of me and I tried to sit up but he shoved me back down roughly, and I hit my head hard enough on the back of the headboard my teeth rattled.

"Don't move," he growled, stabbing the air between us.

But I did. I was not going to be his victim. Not anymore. He was several feet away from me, if I could just get away...

This time when he lunged at me, to shove me back down onto the bed, I dodged out of his way. I bolted for the door, but he caught me by my hair, yanking me backward. I teetered on my heels, but lost my footing and fell hard on my ass. Not expecting me to fall, he stumbled slightly, but didn't crash.

I quickly rolled over and leapt back up to my feet, trying to run again, but he grabbed me by the arm and whipped me around. My foot caught on the decorative carpet and I fell again, but this time, my head hit the ground making an awful cracking sound, with a deafening echo.

I blinked, but I couldn't see. The room was dark, and then Steven's voice, telling me to get up, to move my lazy ass, slowly faded, too.

I guess I was going to get my wish, and death would be mine after all.

LOGAN

I OPENED MY EYES, THE PAIN IN MY SKULL A DISTANT THUD. I couldn't hear the moans and sighs of my friends as they made love. Nor the rustle of the trees overhead. All around me was white, like thick clouds. As though I slept in a cloud. The ground was white. The sky was white. The very air was white.

I sat up, rubbing my temples, but the dull ache didn't fade. Climbing to my feet, I turned in a circle as the white slowly faded and my surroundings became clear.

'Twas night.

I blinked. What in bloody hell? I'd never seen this place before.

I was inside a small, fenced-in enclosure. Short, oddly created buildings loomed at my back and several more beyond the one in front of me, which seemed to be somehow attached to this wooden fence—a poor excuse for a wall.

Was this a village of some sort?

Several lounge chairs littered a stone floor. The only things recognizable to me were the grass and the wood.

"Oh, shit," I muttered, and whirled in a circle looking for them and not seeing them anywhere. "Ewan? Shona?"

No one answered.

"Moira? Rory?"

Still nothing.

Ballocks... I cursed a hundred times when I realized what must have happened.

I'd time traveled, and they were not here with me. Did that mean they'd gone somewhere else, or had they stayed in the glen, in 1544? Lord, I hoped so. Saor needed someone he knew on his side, and I knew those four would protect him with their lives.

But what would happen to me? I wracked my brain for every little thing Emma had ever told me about her modern world.

Shite!

I was in way over my head. And I wasn't going to stay here in this small space. There were two ways out of the fenced enclosure. A glass door leading into the building and a gate around the side.

Considering the glass doors most likely led inside someone's dwelling, and it was the middle of the night, 'twas best if I went out the gate instead.

But taking one step, let alone the dozen or so to the gate, was a task my body seemed resistant, too. My balance was off, and I stumbled and fell with each step.

Nausea swept over me, and I hunched over, vomiting what little contents had rested in my belly.

Perhaps it would be best if I lay down and slept. At least for a few minutes. I'd not be able to find Emma, or even help her when I did, if I couldn't walk without falling or retching.

And so, I laid on one of the oddly shaped lounge chairs. The item more supportive than I thought it would be. But considerably less comfortable than the ones at Castle Gealach.

I stared at the glass door, hoping no one would peek out and see me so close to their hovel, thinking me a thief.

❧ 12 ❧

LOGAN

As soon as I closed my eyes, there was a loud thud from inside the dwelling. A jolt of energy surged through me, protective instincts on high alert.

I sat straight up, blinking and considering my immediate surroundings. Nothing was out of place, and no one came rushing. But who would? Hadn't Emma said in this modern world it seemed that every man, woman and child had to care for themselves? No one, not until the very end, had come to her aid.

I bristled, just remembering the conversations we'd had regarding her life here. My nausea had abated somewhat. Besides, even if I had to hold the bile down, something in my gut told me I needed to go inside the hovel to see what was happening.

It could be that Fate had brought me straight to Emma.

Was it possible this was Shona and Moira's place? There was no way I would know, and only one way to find out.

I crept toward the large glass doors, and tugged at the handle, but it didn't budge initially, then, I was surprised to see that it slid silently to the side, like a secret door.

112

I slipped inside. Taking a moment to steady myself, and acclimate myself to the darkness. Thankfully, the dizziness and nausea had abated. The chamber where I stood was dark, but a light shined through from a room to the right. The walls were lined with wardrobes, and there was a table. It smelled strongly of food, and I suspected this must be a kitchen of some sort, nothing of the likes of which I'd ever seen. I tiptoed quietly toward the lit chamber, to see if someone was there. Looking for any sign of Emma or the people who inhabited this place. But the room was empty. Pictures lined the mantle over the hearth, images of Moira, Shona and others smiling back at me. I was in the right place, I hoped.

Scraping sounds coming from the ceiling had me stopping. Someone was moving around upstairs, but I didn't hear any voices. Just movement.

I didn't call out to alert them of my presence, but moved toward the lit room, in search of stairs. There were none, but a second opening led to what looked like the front entryway, and also the stairs. They were not circular however, but led straight up.

I gripped the hilt of my sword, nerves on high alert and waiting for someone to leap out at me from behind any corner. Thank the saints I'd been fully dressed when I was in the glen. I'd not bothered to remove even my weapons on the off chance I time traveled. Ewan and Shona had never lived down the fact that they journeyed to modern day naked, landing in the middle of a square surrounded by people.

Opting for something subtler, I pulled my *sgian dubh* from my sock, gripping it in my right hand as I rounded the corner. A table by the main door was knocked askew, a vase that had been on top of it had fallen to the floor, shattering in a pile of crystal shards. I avoided the broken pieces, not wanting them to crunch under my boots, warning those above.

Overhead, I could still hear the scuffling sounds amid footsteps, as though someone were dragging something. I closed my eyes, listening harder to see if I could decipher better the size and shape of what was being dragged. A body?

Dear God, was I too late?

Please dinna be Emma.

I tested the strength of the odd, wool covered stairs with my foot. There would be creaks, which would alert whoever it was that I was coming. They could escape out the window.

I ground my teeth with frustration.

Ballocks.

I looked up, ascertaining that the occupied chamber was located in the front, left side room. I could go back outside and scale the wall, climbing in through the window.

They'd not be expecting that. I could take whoever it was by surprise.

I slipped back out through the kitchen and into the yard. Sticking close to the dwelling, I shifted toward the gate, prepared to step through, and then paused. The moon was still high, so most people would be asleep, but it was bright with torches that emitted a false-looking light, and I could be easily spotted if someone were awake.

I'd just have to be careful, and perhaps I'd climb through a window at the rear of the house rather than in the front. Less visible that way.

I looked up; the second story window was about ten feet in the air. The house was made of a stone of sorts, but most of them were flush, not too many handholds as though the mason had purposefully sanded down the stone. That was irritating. And mildly brilliant for fortification's sake.

The window above did have a distinguished ledge. Once I had a grip on that, I could swing up, but how to get the window open? It was covered in a pane of glass.

I shook my head.

Ballocks. Why was this so complicated?

I could easily enter the damn building by opening the door, but scaling it to enter an upper window seemed impossible.

There was no more time to waste. I burst back through the door without a concern for whether or not the person upstairs could hear me. I marched up the stairs and kicked open the door.

Lying on the bed was Emma, knocked unconscious, a bruise marring her pink flesh that I could see visibly in the moonlight. A man, tall and wiry stood over her. My gut twisted, heart wrenched, to see her like that.

As soon as he heard me, he jerked around, a ferocious scowl on his lean face. I knew who it was at once.

Steven.

Muscles taut, prepared to pounce on the bastard, I growled, "Get the hell away from my wife."

Steven snickered. I stuck my *sgian dubh* back in my sock and drew out my sword. I wasn't going to go small with this arsehole. He was going to feel the full force and length of my blade.

"I'm not asking ye twice." My voice was low, full of menace.

Steven's eyes were glued to my sword and he actually had the temerity to look concerned. But then, he grinned, and took a step away, reaching toward his back.

I lunged forward, slicing his arm—not too deep, just a warning slice. I was not waiting for him to bring out whatever weapon he'd use to protect himself. And besides, I thought he deserved death by a thousand cuts.

He yelped, though the wound I'd given him was superficial, and humane, compared to what I wanted to do.

"She was my wife first," the man said, fury dripping from every word. His hands were fisted at his sides and it seemed that his anger had overcome any fear he might have had at my blade.

"I know who ye are." I bared my teeth, letting him know it mattered not.

He cocked his head, surprised. "She told ye about me?"

"Dinna flatter yourself with thinking her words were kind. And be warned, I've been wanting to kill ye for a long time."

This time when Steven reached for his pocket, he leapt back out of my way. Quicker, having learned his lesson. If it was a weapon, it wasn't one I'd ever seen, nor could I decipher just how it was supposed to protect him and harm me. 'Twas a black box. I assumed if he were able to subdue me—which he couldn't—he could simply bludgeon me with it.

"You'll have to catch me first," he said.

And then he was gone from the room, simply disappearing into thin air.

I took a step back. Then a step forward. Turned in a circle. How had he done that? A trick of the eyes?

I dropped to my knees and checked beneath the bed. Opened up a set of doors but all that was in there were clothing type items.

"Where the bloody hell is he?"

The black box... It was a magical weapon of some sort.

"Logan... Is that you?"

Forget Steven, I whipped around to see Emma still prone on the bed.

"Oh, my love." In two strides I was by her side, kneeling on the floor. I brushed the hair from her face feeling a knot on the side of her head. A bruise marred her cheek. "What did he do to ye?"

"I fell..." Her arms rose limply to stroke my face. "Is this another dream? Why do I still hurt? I don't normally hurt in my dreams."

"'Tis not a dream," I whispered, leaning forward and

pressing a kiss to her lips. "I came for ye. We're going to go home."

Her hand moved softly against my body, flattening to my chest, a smile touched her mouth. "You came..."

"Aye. This place is madness."

She laughed quietly. "Where is Saor?"

"He is safe, back at the castle, waiting for ye."

Her eyes widened and she tried to sit up. "Where is Steven?" Panic filled her voice.

Should I tell her the man had simply disappeared into thin air? I had to; she'd been through hell and deserved to know.

"I dinna know." I shook my head, still damned confused. "He pulled a black box from his pocket and next thing I know, he was gone."

"A black box," she murmured. "Mrs. MacDonald had a black box, too."

"MacDonald?" I leapt to my feet. "Where is she? I'll skin her alive."

Emma sat up straighter, reaching for me. "No, no, Logan, she's gone. Same black box."

I knelt back by her side, cradling her body against mine. "I dinna understand. What is the black box?"

"I think it's a device. A time traveling tool. There was a man, an elderly gentleman, that said he was Moira and Shona's guardian. He told me there are time jumpers. That the Ayreshire lassies are in trouble."

"Time jumpers?" I shook my head. This was a lot of information to take in and I wasn't certain I understood all of it.

"Aye. We need to go. We need to get back to them. We have to protect them from whomever is coming for them."

"Do ye have a black box?"

She shook her head. "No."

"How do we get one?"

Emma tried to swing her legs over the side of the bed, and I helped her. She winced and squeezed her eyes shut.

"Och, love I wish I could take away your pain. Are there any herbals here? I could fetch ye some."

"I need an aspirin," she moaned. "My head hurts."

"Aspirin? What's that? Is that how we get a black box?"

She smiled and shook her head, then said, "Ouch," pressing her hand to the side where the nasty knot was.

Ballocks, but I'd rip the black box from Steven's hands and shred him to pieces the next time I laid my eyes on him. Bastard had slipped right through my fingers.

"It's medicine," she explained. "Modern medicine."

"I'll get it. Where is it?"

"Maybe in the bathroom?"

"There's a room dedicated to baths? Why would there be medicine in there?" I held the back of my hand to her forehead. "Are ye feeling all right?"

She giggled. "Yes, I'll be fine. Just a headache. Help me up." Then she leaned against me, pressing her head to my chest. "I missed you, Logan. I know this world is crazy, and you don't understand a lot of it, but I'm so grateful you came for me."

"Och, my love, I couldn't let ye languish. I had to find ye." I wrapped an arm around her shoulders and kissed the top of her head. "Tell me where to go."

She pointed toward the entrance to the chamber and I walked her back out into the corridor. "There." She pointed toward a door in the center of the hallway.

We walked to another smaller chamber with a white marble-looking chair and a... "Is that a tub?"

It was small, only big enough to hold a bairn. And also made of white marble-like material.

"A sink."

I grunted.

"That's the tub." She pointed behind her and I saw a large white tub built into the wall. "This is a toilet, like a chamber pot."

I glanced at the odd chair.

I frowned, confused. "Who would wash where they shite?"

Emma laughed. "A good question."

She flicked on a light and I jumped back.

"Holy Mother..."

Emma grinned. "They don't use candles so much in the modern era. There's a thing called electricity. An energy that powers many things."

And then she confused me more by pulling a reflecting glass away from the wall and revealing a secret set of shelves with tiny, oddly colored bottles.

She opened one and dumped tiny red balls into her hand. Then she turned a nozzle and water shot from a tiny well-like tube.

"This world is..." I couldn't put a word to it. In fact, it was overwhelming enough that I, too, was starting to get a headache.

"Can I have one of those, my head is starting to ache."

"A pill?" She glanced at me in the mirror, something that was so foreign to me, but she seemed completely at ease with it.

"The medicine?" I pointed toward the bottle.

She nodded and handed me a couple. "You'll need more than one."

I put them in my mouth, biting down, and the bitterness of it washing over my tongue making me shudder.

She handed me a cup. "I don't usually chew them. Just swallow them whole."

How had Rory become accustomed to all this? I swished

the water around the bitter powder in my mouth and swallowed, hoping to never taste that again.

"I think we should find out where Mr. McAlister either lives or works and go there. We need to see if he has a black box."

"Whose croft is this?" I asked.

"Moira and Shona's."

"That is what I suspected, but, how did Steven get here?"

Emma let out a long sigh. "Apparently he befriended a time jumper and she lured me into her home and care. I asked her to bring me here. When I laid down, she must have told Steven where I was."

"Are ye a time jumper?"

She shook her head and wrapped her arms around my waist, resting her head over my heart. It felt so good to hold her. I cupped the back of her head, stroking her soft, wild locks.

"I missed you so much," she said. "And I tried to be strong but..."

"Ye were strong."

"No. I wasn't. He overpowered me." Her voice broke.

I tried to soothe her, reminding her that, "Being strong isn't always about physical strength."

"I know... But I thought I could get away from him." She held her head back, fixing her eyes on mine. "I actually thought I could."

"Sometimes being strong is about surviving. Remember when MacDonald took me? I was unable to overpower the men. But I survived."

She nodded, her entire body shuddering.

"I'm so glad you're here. How is Saor?"

"The bairn is stubborn, just like ye." I chuckled. "He's doing just fine. I can tell he misses ye though. He's been more quiet of late, as though he's listening, waiting to hear your voice."

"I want to go home."

"Me, too."

"How did you come here? Maybe we can try that to get back to your time."

I shook my head, chuckled. "That is impossible."

"Why?" She looked at me, puzzled.

I explained the "orgy" in the glen, and she gasped, laughter in her eyes.

"Is it too much to hope they'll simply stay there until we return?" she asked with a skeptical laugh. "So absorbed with lust, maybe?"

"They might. Mayhap we should... try it."

"Make love?"

"Aye. If the power of it brought me here, maybe it can take us back, and then we won't need to find the black box."

She walked her fingers over my chest to my neck, stroking the stubble on my chin. "I think it's worth a try."

"What about your head? And your face..." Studying the bruise on her cheek I was once more filled with a burning rage. "When I get my hands on that bastard..."

She cupped my hand to her face, and then kissed my palm. "I feel fine. More than fine. Better than fine. And I want to be close to you, in the flesh."

I lifted her up in my arms and carried her back toward the chamber we'd just vacated.

"Not that one," she said. "I don't want to be in the one where *he* was."

"As ye wish, my love."

13

EMMA

In Logan's arms, the headache that had blurred my vision eased, and memories of Steven's assault were washed away. My husband had my full attention. The fire in his dark eyes, the chisel of his features, every line and ridge of his solid body.

He closed the door, shutting us away from the craziness of this world and the next. Laying me down gently on the bed, he stretched out beside me, and though we weren't at Gealach, I felt so much closer to home. He leaned on one elbow, his free hand tracing a circle on my belly. I watched his tender movements, leaning in as he stroked my cheek, then the line of my jaw.

Our eyes were locked on one another, so much unsaid, but powerfully evident in our gazes. We'd almost lost each other.

"I love you," I said, cupping his hand to my face. "So much."

"I love ye, too, *mo chridhe*."

His heart. I was his heart and he was mine.

I leaned up at the same time he leaned down, our lips finally touching. His mouth was firm, but velvet soft, and even after kissing him hundreds, thousands of times, his lips still had the ability to spark a storm of butterflies in my belly and tingles throughout my limbs.

I rolled onto my side, curling a leg over top of his, my arm around his back tugging him closer to me. His heat sank into my skin in a wave of decadent, blissful pleasure.

We normally played so many games in bed. Who was dominant, who was submissive, who was going to win, and who was going to be the infinitely pleasured loser? But tonight, I didn't want to play games. Tonight, I just wanted to be loved, and love in return. To leisurely explore. To kiss forever and ever. To make love slowly. Deliciously intoxicated by his touch.

Logan seemed to sense this, or maybe it was what he wanted, too, because he stroked my cheek, rocked his body against mine and kissed me with such passion I could barely breathe. But, he didn't taunt me. He didn't tease me like he normally did. No, he gave, and gave and gave, and he seized what I offered in return.

I trembled with nerves, with excitement, with emotion, and I realized, as Logan's hand stroked over my shoulder, down my arm and around the small of my back, that he, too, was trembling.

We'd not made love—except in the dream—since before I'd birthed Saor, and the nine months prior to that had been an adventure in seeing what position worked best with my growing belly. In reality it had been nearly a year since my body had been my own, and that we'd made love with nothing between us but sweat.

I was changed, fuller, softer. And for the briefest of moments when his hand curled over my hip, I worried that he wouldn't like the way I'd changed. However, I worried needlessly. Logan gripped me tighter and groaned against my lips, his cock full and pressed urgently to my lower belly.

I shifted, pulling myself a little higher so that I could press that hard strength more fully between my legs.

The fabric of the black dress I sported was thinner than the gowns I wore in 1544, allowing me to feel his potent erection more fully. I gasped.

The sudden spark of need that filled me had me nearly wrenching up his kilt, my dress, and getting to business, but I didn't want it to be so fast. I wanted to cherish these precious moments together, because I didn't know how long they would last—we could be transported back in time at any moment. And most of all, because I didn't know when I'd get them again.

Logan's hand caressed down my thigh to the ticklish spot behind my knee, over my calf and to my shoe, which he flipped off, letting it fall to the floor with a small thud.

He massaged his way back up to my hip and then over to my behind, cupping its roundness and massaging it, all the while moaning against me, making me shiver with delight.

"Ye've always had the most beautiful arse," he whispered, tugging at my lower lip with his teeth.

And then he was rolling me onto my belly and trailing kisses over the back of my neck, his fingers forging a path down my spine to the hem of my dress.

He slowly pulled the hem up over my thighs, until my buttocks were exposed—along with the high-cut practical panties I was wearing. He skimmed a finger beneath the elastic, and I held my breath at his touch.

Logan leaned down, pulling the dress higher and pressed a kiss at my lower spine.

"There are no buttons. How do I take this off?" he asked, his voice gravely, husky. "'Tis more like a shift, is it not?"

I laughed. "There is a tie in the front."

"A tie? That is all?" He sounded shocked.

I nodded, and rolled onto my side, tugging at the knot, while I laughed.

"Ah." Logan wiggled his brows. "Verra easy to access."

"Very." I smiled and his fingers tangled with mine as we both rushed to get the dress untied.

His mouth claimed mine as we finally saw the task handled, the air in the room hitting the skin of my stomach.

I teased his lower lip with my tongue, gulping air when his tongue slid over mine. Amazing that feeling, velvet soft and slick, how it sparked awareness over every inch of my skin.

Logan's hand pressed flat to my belly then caressed upward to my breasts, full in a matching practical bra.

"And this... How do I get rid of this?" he teased, skimming is fingers behind the fabric to stroke my hardened nipples.

"Wait," I said, clasping his hand to my breast with his hand over it. "Maybe we shouldn't..."

I was still self-conscious of them, having only been used to feeding our child, it felt... awkward.

"Dinna be shy," he said, kissing near my ear and then sliding his lips along the column of my neck. "I love your breasts."

"But—"

"Shh..." He kissed my collarbone and I shivered at the sensual scratch of his stubble on my sensitive skin.

Logan roved lower, his breath hot on my skin. And I quivered with pleasure. He teased the fabric of the bra with his tongue, tugging at it with his teeth until one nipple was exposed.

I groaned, arching my back, as his lips brushed the taut peak. Amazing how versatile the body was. Made for creating and giving life. Made for giving and receiving pleasure.

I could barely breathe, air passing back forth through my lips in gasps and sighs. I tugged at the pin on his shoulder, letting it fall to wherever my shoe was. I pulled his shirt from his kilt, sliding my hand over the hot, rigid muscles of his back, tracing scars I'd kissed a hundred times.

"I want to feel you," I said, gripping his belt. "Skin to skin."

I itched to be naked with him. To rub our bodies together, to feel the hair of his chest tickle my breasts, the hair of his legs teasing my inner thighs.

I tugged on the belt, feeling it release. I slid it from around his body and tossed it.

"Unwrap me," he teased.

"Oh, I've been wanting to do that for a long time."

He leaned back on his heels and I tugged at the fabric, around and around his hips, until finally his turgid flesh was exposed. Long, thick, a vein throbbing down the center.

"God it's been so long," I said.

"Worth the wait," he murmured, scooting closer on his knees.

He took hold of my dress at the shoulders and pulled it the rest of the way off. Tugged at my panties, slipping them over my hips, down my thighs, my calves, ankles and flinging them. Then, he fingered the bra.

"This, too," he said.

I nodded, no longer caring, but needing to feel him on me.

I reached behind and unhooked the bra. I kicked off my other shoe, our clothes in a heap on the floor.

With Logan kneeling between my thighs, I pressed my hand to the place over his heart.

"We belong together," I said. "That's why you're here. I should never have left."

"'Twasn't your choice."

"I know, and you were right when you said Fate made a mistake."

"Dinna leave me, ever."

"Never of my own volition."

I skimmed my hand lower, loving the ridges of his muscles, the hardness of his belly, until I reached his throbbing cock. I wrapped my fingers around him, just as I'd done a thousand times before, but still, the silky hardness of him sent shivers racing all over me.

Logan's head fell back as I stroked my hand upward, over the thick head and then back down.

"This will not last long if ye keep that up, love. Ye've got the magic touch."

I giggled. "So I shouldn't do this?" Before he could stop me, I spread my legs wider and leaned down low, slicking my tongue around his cockhead, lapping up the drop of fluid at the center.

"Ballocks, lass, nay..."

But he didn't stop me. In fact, his hips jerked forward, a silent invitation to continue. I wrapped my lips around him and sucked just the tip, teasing him, my hand still at the base.

Logan moaned, deep and guttural, his hand threading through my hair. I teased and teased, and then finally drew him in deep. His entire body shuddered and I was reminded of why I liked to play power games with him. Because I liked that feeling of knowing he was at my mercy, that I was giving him so much pleasure he, the mighty warrior, was trembling on his knees.

"No more," he growled, tugging at my hair until I let go.

He lifted me at my waist and I wrapped my legs around him, my arms around his shoulders. He knelt back on his heels. His cock stood tall and slick and pulsing between our bodies.

"I need to be inside ye," he said. "Right now."

I gripped his erection, and titled my hips forward, lifting enough to press his cockhead at my entrance.

"What's stopping you?"

"Good heavens, lassie, nothing."

He pumped his hips forward, invading my body and I enthusiastically surrendered. Despite the slickness of my desire, there was a slight pinch, as though I were a virgin all over again after having birthed our son. I gasped, but the pain was quickly gone, replaced with an urgent need.

Oh, but it was sweet. That feeling of being filled, stretched.

"Holy fu..." I cut off Logan's curse by claiming his mouth with mine, tangling our tongues, and moaning at the exquisite sensation of our bodies finally being connected in the flesh.

His hands guided my hips in a slow, rocking motion. I gripped his shoulders, nails digging in. Intense pleasure filled me, every muscle in my body on alert. Every nerve firing.

Hips rocking, pelvis thrusting, we were completely oblivious to anything other than giving each other pleasure. Finding release.

"I missed ye," he murmured against my mouth.

"I missed you more," I moaned.

Pleasure built, gripping me from the inside, I was so close...

"Don't stop," I demanded.

"Saints," Logan moaned.

I rocked back and forth, harder, faster, and he kept pace, thrusting deep. The tremors of my orgasm started, faint and then came pounding, jolting. I clung to him as my body broke apart, pleasure radiating. I cried out, squeezing him tight as I rode the waves, rode his cock.

Logan growled, fingers digging into my hips as he thrust home a few more times, pulsing his own release inside me.

I wrapped my arms around his neck, and held onto him, even as my breathing returned to normal, my heartbeat slowed. I couldn't let go. And he held me tight, too. Unmoving. We could have stayed like that all night.

"Well, finally. I thought ye'd be at it all night."

The light in the bedroom flicked on. I leapt backward, falling from Logan's lap to see the door wide open and Mrs. MacDonald standing in the doorway, her black box in one hand and a gun in the other.

❧ 14 ❧

LOGAN

I leapt from the bed, holding my hands out to block Emma from the elderly woman holding a miniature canon in one hand and the same black box I'd seen Steven handling, in the other.

"Who in bloody hell are ye?" I bellowed.

She gazed at me with contempt, her lackluster eyes roaming down and then up the front of my body.

"Does it truly matter?" she asked.

"Damned right it does," I said through bared teeth. "Ye've barged into our chamber, interrupted a verra private moment, not to mention the canon ye've got pointed our way."

"That's Mrs. MacDonald," Emma said from behind me, her fingers gently stroking my back.

The older woman grunted, her eyes narrowing. She didn't seem the least bit fazed by my wrath. What game did she play?

"Tell your blustering lover I'm harmless," Mrs. MacDonald said, though the wry smile on her face said otherwise.

"He is my husband," Emma said proudly.

"Anyone with the name MacDonald is an enemy of mine." I glanced toward the floor, my sword only a few feet in front. Would it be enough time for her to light the fuse at the end of her small canon? For that was the way she'd fire it, was it not? I prayed it was...

"She has a gun," Emma murmured. "They are deadly, Logan."

Mrs. MacDonald snickered. "That's right. Ye've never seen one of these have ye?" She pointed the canon—gun?—toward the corner of the room, twitched her finger, which was followed by a loud thunder cracking the air in the room. The floor in the corner erupted into splinters of wood and carpet.

"What the—" But my surprise was short lived as I realized that very deadly canon-gun did not need to be lit, but could apparently be fired by a mere twitch of a finger.

An enemy wasn't even given a chance to protect themselves. The way it had splintered the wood, a shield wouldn't help. What had the modern world come to?

Mrs. MacDonald waved the gun toward me, her lips pulled back in a snarl. I held my arms out to the side, protectively blocking Emma.

"I have no qualms shooting ye right in the head"—she looked down at my groin and jutted her chin—"either one."

Damn. How was I supposed to fight with the weapon she had? With a twitch of her finger she'd blow my fucking ballocks off.

I held out my arms in surrender, took a slow step forward and smiled at her. Seemed my wits were going to be the best weapon in disarming her right now. If I could get close enough to remove the bloody thing from her gnarled fingers.

"If we could just talk," I started, but she cut me off.

"Stop right there." Mrs. MacDonald blew out a disgusted snort, and rolled her eyes away from me. "Put some damned clothes on."

"Lower your weapon." My voice was firm but still congenial.

She raised a brow. "Not likely to happen."

"I'll put on some clothes if ye only lower it a moment."

She rolled her eyes. "I have a mind to blow ye to smithereens before ye get the chance."

"Mrs. MacDonald." Emma managed to scoot around me before I could hold her back.

My beautiful wife was already dressed in the black gown she'd worn earlier, though the way her breasts moved with the fabric, I could tell she'd not bothered with the heinous contraption she called a bra, thank the saints. She held up her hands. "Please. I don't know what's going on. But you helped me before. I trusted you. What's changed? Is it money? How can I change your mind?"

Mrs. MacDonald made a *tsking* sound with her tongue, shaking her head as though Emma had just taken the last honey-cake from the buttery. "Nothing's changed, my dear. And no amount of coin could keep me from my task. As for trusting me, well, your mistake. Steven said you were too dumb for your own good. He said taking you would be easy. Little did he know I have friends in high places." She grinned at me. "Rather familial, really."

Bloody hell. Chief MacDonald, Lord of the Isles, could get to us even here.

I could tell by the small pulse in her jaw that Emma was angry, but she kept a smile on her face belying her true emotions. I was so damned proud of her. The lass was strong, confident. A force to be reckoned with. When we were done with the old crone, I'd kneel at Emma's feet and tell her as much.

"Maybe I am dumb," Emma said with a shrug. "Or *maybe* you really did want to help me."

"Ha." Mrs. MacDonald waved the gun toward Emma and I leapt in front of her. "Och, posh, get away from her. I'm not going to shoot the lass. I *need* her."

I didn't move. "I will not allow ye to harm my wife."

"My orders are for ye, Highlander. Now put some bloody clothes on before I'm forced to mar your very muscular and golden skin."

Emma faced me, pleading in her eyes. I wished at that moment our magic had given us the ability to hear each other's thoughts. But I suppose it didn't truly matter, I could read them well enough on her face. Her eyes were slightly wider, her lips trembling in a straight line as she tried to smile, but couldn't. Her skin was pale, and that vein in the side of her neck that pulsed hard when she was unnerved was going wild.

"Only because I dinna want ye staring at my cock any longer." I bent to pick up my shirt and plaid. I pulled on my *leine* and then roughly pleated my plaid before wrapping it around my waist. Didn't need a faulty pleat to ruin any chance I had to subdue the bitch. I secured my belt—weapons clinking as I did so.

"Remove your weapons," Mrs. MacDonald said.

I shook my head, baring my teeth. "If ye get to keep yours, I'll be keeping mine."

"I'll shoot ye on the count of three if ye dinna set them aside, ye jackanapes."

I bristled at the insult. If one of us was a jackanapes, it was she. "What does it matter?" I ground out. "I'd not be able to wrench out my sword and use it against ye before ye got off a shot."

"Even still." Mrs. MacDonald shrugged.

Did that mean she thought I might be able to? If she

made even the slightest turn away from me, or dropped her gaze for a second, I was confident I could.

Slowly, eyes steady on the wretched woman, I pulled out my sword, the steel gleaming in the light. I challenged her with my gaze, and she cocked back the piece of the canon that I wasn't ignorant enough to ignore. She was going to fire.

"I'm putting it down," I said, slowly placing the sword on the floor at my feet.

"Your *sgian dubh*, too," she said, pointing at the spot beneath my sock where it bulged.

I nodded, pulling it out and tossing it to the floor.

She'd not seen the second one sewn into the lining of my plaid, and I sent up a silent prayer of thanksgiving for that. I was not completely weaponless.

"Put on your shoes, prissy pants." Mrs. MacDonald waved the gun at Emma and then toward one of her shoes on the floor. "We're going for a walk."

"Where to?" Emma asked, reading my mind.

"Somewhere," was all the crone said.

Like hell I was going *somewhere* with this madwoman, but before I could speak, Emma had already begun.

"What happened?" Emma slipped into her shoes, keeping her gaze steady on our captor. "Where is Mr. McAlister? And Steven?"

Mrs. MacDonald narrowed her eyes, though there was a flicker of something beyond annoyance at us stalling her. "I have no idea. Let's go."

Emma shook her head, refusing to budge. "But, wait, how can you have no idea?"

That same flicker returned. "Just as I said, I've no idea."

That was the reason for her irritation. She didn't know where they were or when they'd come back. There was some part of this plot that was out of her miserable control.

"So there isn't some sort of time jumper's headquarters or someone you check in with? Like a handler or a pimp?"

I snickered at that last one, and winked at my wife. She was asking legitimate questions and getting a barb in there, too. I crossed my arms over my chest and waited to see just how this was going to play out.

Mrs. MacDonald let out a short bark of laughter, rolling her eyes as though Emma were the biggest idiot in all of Scotland. "Oh, honey, ye've so much to learn."

Emma put her hands on her hips, cocked her head and jutted her chin. God, how I loved her strength.

"And I've time to learn it right now."

Mrs. MacDonald shook her head, pursed her lips, returning just as much attitude as she was receiving. "Ye dinna actually. Out." She waved the gun toward the door. "I will follow the both of ye downstairs."

Emma glanced at me, and I indicated she should go first. I'd put myself between the two women. Emma nodded and I followed her to the door, ducking beneath the frame. She walked slowly, methodically, buying us both some time to figure out a way to stall the crazed woman.

"You still didn't tell me what happened. I thought I heard you fighting with Mr. McAlister," Emma said as we walked.

The barrel of the gun poked into the middle of my spine. Mrs. MacDonald was very close behind me. If I fell backward on her, as we descended the stairs, there might be enough time for Emma to get away. The woman would be stuck beneath my weight—my *dead* weight, as the sudden fall would likely cause her trigger finger to pull.

But it was worth it. I'd gladly give up my life to save my wife's. And then she could steal the black box from Mrs. MacDonald's crushed body and return to our son.

"We were fighting," Mrs. MacDonald said.

Emma paused on the stairs to straighten a framed portrait along the wall leading down, and I also stopped in turn. The faces of Moira and Shona stared back at us from behind glass.

"But why?" Emma asked. "I thought the two of you were on the same side."

Again, the gun poked into my back, but I didn't budge. I wasn't going to run my wife over. Not a chance in hell.

"I am on nobody's side," Mrs. MacDonald said. "Especially not *that* idiot."

There was such derision in her tone. I wanted to meet the man who seemed less worthy of her respect than even me. I chanced a glance behind me to see the old crone's scowl.

"Idiot?" Emma clucked her tongue and continued down the stairs, and I followed. "Mr. McAlister seemed pretty smart to me."

Another groan from the wench. "He knows next to nothing. The man is a glorified babysitter."

"Has he more than one charge?" I asked.

"The twins, ye dimwit."

Shona and Moira. This man was their guardian. No wonder the MacDonald woman didn't like him. He was protecting yet more treasures their blasted kin couldn't get their hands on.

"More than they?" I asked out of curiosity. Just how many secret babies were there in the realm, spanning hundreds of years?

"I'll not be telling ye that," she bit out sourly.

"What will ye be telling us?" I asked, unable to hide my impatience. "Perhaps how that little black box works?"

Mrs. MacDonald laughed. "So ye know about the box."

I shrugged, and ignored the glare from Emma.

"Well, ye were holding it very obviously in the chamber up there. 'Tis fascinating," I said. "That ye simply turn a wheel—"

"A wheel?" Mrs. MacDonald scoffed.

"Well, I dinna know the name for things here..." I trailed off, hoping she'd just fill in the blanks, where my pretended ignorance bloomed. For certes, I didn't know the names of everything, but I most assuredly didn't know how to use that damn box, and if I had to use trickery to get the answers, then so be it.

"Button." I could practically *hear* the roll of her eyes. Little did she know the jest was on her. "And ye press it, not turn it."

I kept up the dumb act, finding it quite entertaining that she was falling for my ruse. "But how do ye make sure ye get to where ye want to go? That is just amazing... Do ye will it with your mind?"

"Ye punch it in, dimwit. It's a computer."

"A computer?" I paused on the stairs, her language completely lost on me now, but I prayed Emma was picking up on it, because if I could steal that box, then Emma could take us to where we needed to go. Or at the very least, take herself.

"Don't even ask," Mrs. MacDonald spewed. "Ye'll never understand. Keep moving."

I should fall on her now. Wrestle the bitch to the ground. She was old, weak. My reflexes were quick, swifter than hers, I'd be willing to bet all my lands on that.

Once Emma had reached the bottom, she turned to face me and I winked, nodded my head only the slightest bit so as not to draw attention. She seemed to understand enough to scoot toward the main door and out of the way.

Without warning, I whipped around, staring the old bat right in her widened, surprised eyes. With one hand, I grabbed Mrs. MacDonald's right wrist which held the gun and with my other, I grabbed her left. I squeezed, watching pain and frustration fill her face, until she let go of the weapon and the black box, both of them bouncing down the stairs. Emma moved quickly to pick them up.

"Ye see," I said low, and in her face. "I couldn't let ye get away with whatever it was ye were planning. They dinna call me the Guardian for no reason. I *am* the Guardian of Scotland, and ye are nothing but a conniving old bitch. If ye knew anything, ye'd know I'd bested your clan a hundred times."

Her old wrinkled lips pursed angrily, and hatred, pure and vile screamed from her eyes.

"No matter where ye are, ye'll never be safe from me and the others," she said.

"Nay," I drawled out. "Ye've got the wrong of it, crone. *Ye'll* never be safe from *me*." I grinned, the kind I often gave men in battle just before I brought down a final blow upon their skulls. "At least, for as long as I let ye live."

She seemed surprised; perhaps thinking I would kill her right then and there, but I was against violence towards women and the elderly, and she'd not tried to kill us yet, so she had that on her side. Though I ought to break her hand for considering blowing off my ballocks. I'd show her mercy, something I'd found hard to do with anyone carrying the same name.

"Go back to your hovel, wherever that might be. Live out the rest of your life in peace." I doubted she would take my suggestion.

"Go to hell," she spat through gritted teeth.

Just as I suspected. Stubborn as a goat.

"Mrs. MacDonald," Emma said. "Where is your car?"

Car? What the hell was a car? I seemed to recall Emma telling me about it once, but it was hard to match the foreign words with the actual objects.

"Why should I tell ye that?" The older woman jutted her chin obstinately, still struggling in my grasp.

"Because, if you don't, I will shoot you." Emma's face was calm, serious. "Shooting you doesn't mean you have to die."

"Ye wouldn't," Mrs. MacDonald said.

Emma lowered the gun, pointing at the woman's foot. "Oh, I would. I've a greater reason to be rid of you and on my way than you have to keep me here."

Emma pulled back the lever; the same one Mrs. MacDonald had cocked before shooting the corner of the bedchamber.

I held my tongue, allowing her to make these decisions. Emma had been the one tormented by this woman and if she really wanted to shoot her, I was going to fully support her choice.

"'Tis outside."

Emma opened the door a crack, and then nodded. "I'm shocked. You didn't lie."

Mrs. MacDonald huffed.

"Well," Emma said, pursing her lips. "I do apologize for this in advance, it's going to hurt."

And then she pulled the trigger, shooting Mrs. MacDonald in the foot.

The woman screamed and I jumped just the smallest bit. I'd not expected her to go through with it. The woman fell to the floor, blood seeping from the hole in her shoe.

"Never get in the way of a mother and her child," Emma said. "As a mother, I'm sure you understand."

Emma still held the gun pointed at the old crone, but she turned her gaze to stare at me wide-eyed. Time to go. Time for me to step in and give her the strength she needed. I nodded, mouthed, *well done*. I'd hug her as soon as we were out of sight.

"Ye bitch!" Mrs. MacDonald shouted from the floor where she sat, hugging her foot to her chest.

"How can I help?" I asked Emma.

"Wait here. Watch her."

I did as she asked while Emma ran back upstairs, returning with a small satchel and my weapons. I sheathed my sword and returned my sgian dubh to my sock, watching her hurry toward the kitchen. Once back, I noted she'd shoved the gun into her bag, along with the black box. She then reached down and rummaged through Mrs. MacDonald's clothes all while Mrs. MacDonald attempted to swat her away. Emma pulled out several items, and seeming satisfied, shoved them into the bag, too.

"Come on. We need to go now, before someone comes to see what happened." She opened the door and I checked the surroundings.

"All clear," I said.

"This way." Emma leaned against me for a half second, though I could tell she wanted to do so longer.

She pointed to a large steel box that sat on the edge of the road, with wheels made of an odd material.

"A car," I mused, remembering what she'd told me about vehicles.

"Yes. Get in." She rushed around to the other side and opened the side of it, her eyes meeting mine. "Here."

I hurried to do her bidding, managing to fold myself up enough once seated on the cushioned chair. Lord, but it was uncomfortable for a man my size.

Emma came around the other side, sat down, and plugged in the key and the whole thing rumbled to life.

"Remember what I said about cars?" she asked. "You may want to lay back and close your eyes. You're likely to get sick."

"I'm certain I've experienced things far more disturbing then this," I assured her with a wink.

She smiled, and the vehicle lurched forward.

I grabbed on for dear life, swallowing down the bile rising up my throat, because she didn't slow down, if anything, my sweet wife sped up.

❧ 15 ❧

MOIRA

I walked the length of the great hall at Gealach with the young heir, Saor, cradled in my arms. A tuft of fiery-red hair on his otherwise bald scalp. He gurgled and squirmed, cheeks fat and rosy, eyes as blue as the sky, looking genuinely content one moment and quite irritated with me the next.

I smiled and cooed at him, and for one so young, he had a surprisingly genuine smile. Not gas or dreams, but the grin of a babe well cared for and loved.

It'd been a week since Logan had vanished from the glen, though we all knew just where he'd gone. Or at least, we *hoped* we knew where he was. Nothing was ever a certainty. And I prayed daily that he knew *who* he was. When Shona and Ewan had both come to the 1500's neither of them knew who they were in their past life. It took Shona five years before she remembered, and Ewan took nearly twenty years to recall his past. If Logan forgot who he was, it would be a disaster for everyone, even if he only lost his memory for a few short weeks.

He was our leader. The guardian of our country. The

keeper of crown secrets. The protector of many. I shuddered to think what would happen should he forget.

"How is the bairn?" Rory asked.

I looked up at him, watching him approach, kilt swaying, and muscular legs marching toward me.

"He is very happy," I said, wondering if at that moment a bairn of my own was growing inside me.

Rory tickled Saor's chin. "He looks it."

Though Rory had a son of his own already, I knew he couldn't wait to have a child who he could raise, who he could love from birth—not to mention, that this child wouldn't want to murder him.

"Rory," Ewan said, striding into the hall, his brow furrowed, hand on his sword hilt as though he expected trouble at any moment.

My belly flopped. Ewan often looked disturbed, and I couldn't blame him, but he looked even more agitated than usual.

"What is it?" Rory asked, his tone conveying he felt the same as I.

"There's a man here..." Ewan glanced behind himself. The warrior was positively skittish. "From, ye know..."

"Really?" I gasped, peering around him. "Someone new?"

Ewan's brows drew so low, they almost connected. "Aye. Appeared out of blasted nowhere. Scared the shite out of me. Pardon my language, Moira."

"'Tis no bother, I've heard worse," I murmured, thinking of all the heinous things Dickie, my ex-boyfriend, had said. And more recently, the vile things Ranulf had spewed.

"He is waiting in the entryway. Guards are with him," Ewan said.

"Who is he? Who is he asking for?" Rory asked.

"He's asking for Logan. Said his name was McAlister."

"I dinna know any McAlisters," Rory said.

"Neither do I," Ewan replied.

Well, *they* might not know a McAlister, but I did. The blood drained from my face, and I swayed slightly on my feet, clutching onto Saor a little tighter.

Both men looked my way, alarmed.

"McAlister?" I said, faintly.

"Aye." Ewan stepped forward, as did the nursemaid who'd been hovering nearby.

She took Saor from my grasp; thank the heavens, as I was feeling so faint... I touched the back of my hand to my forehead.

"'Tis familiar to ye?" Rory slid an arm around my back, steadying me, and I leaned against his solid form.

I nodded. "Where is Shona?" I pressed my hands to my temple. "I need my sister. She needs to be here."

The truth was, I did know a McAlister. He was our solicitor in Edinburgh. The one in charge of our estate, our finances, our well-being. He'd been around since we were babies. He was like a grandfather to us. The one who set up the various foster homes, and saved us from the very same ones. Though he never took us in himself, something about that not being what was written in their parents' directive.

I instructed the nursemaid to take Saor upstairs while we waited for Ewan and Shona.

Once she was gone, I tried to gather my thoughts. "Rory, if he's who I think he is, then he is welcome, but the reason he's here cannot be good."

And just how had he come to be here? Was this a result of Logan having traveled to the future? It did seem as though if one went, another came and vice versa.

Ewan rushed away in search of Shona, while I tried to steady the rapid beat of my heart.

"Moira, tell me what's going on," Rory murmured against my ear, soft and comforting. A pillar of strength, always.

I explained who I thought McAlister could be.

"But... how would he know ye're here?"

"I can only imagine that he must have spoken with Emma."

"That means she was in Edinburgh."

I nodded. "We'll only know for certain if we talk to him."

"We canna speak with him here." Rory went to the grand trestle table and poured me a glass of watered wine.

"Nor Logan's library," I said, knowing how well the Guardian of Scotland protected his documents. I took a sip, feeling both relieved and guilty. If I were pregnant, would the wine harm a child? Then again, it was very watered down. And how many of the women here only drank ale or wine? Ugh! I couldn't be worrying over this now, when an even more potential disaster was on our hands. I pressed my hand to my belly, unable to stop myself. Didn't matter the disaster, I was still curious.

"Ewan will know where to go," Rory said softly. "Are ye all right? Are ye feeling better?"

I shook my head, and then nodded. "I'll be fine."

He pulled me into his arms, and we both stayed like that, my eyes closed, nose buried in his chest. My heart started to beat normally again and I pulled back a moment to stare up into his eyes.

"I love you," I said.

"I love ye, too."

I could hear the tapping of my sister's shoes as she ran, before she even appeared. And I'd give her a strong talking to, considering she was nearing her due date. Shona burst into the great hall, a flurry of plaid skirts and dark, unruly hair.

"Is it true?" she asked, grabbing hold of my arms and looking into my eyes.

"You shouldn't be running," I said.

"I told her the verra same thing," Ewan said, running in behind her.

She waved away our comments.

I stared into her face, so like my own, and nodded.

"This can't be good," she whispered.

"I agree."

"Where can we talk with this McAlister fellow?" Rory asked Ewan.

"There is a chamber Logan set aside especially for such meetings. I'll take ye there and then fetch the man."

We followed him from the great hall, and down the corridor past Logan's office. Not too far, Ewan opened a door that led to a fairly plain room, but large. In the center of the room was a long trestle table, cleared of anything but three candelabras fitted with candles that had yet to be lit.

The walls were adorned with simple tapestries that showed no hint of politics or religion. Landscapes. A unicorn. A sideboard held a variety of decanters and cups. The hearth was cleaned of all ashes, fresh wood stacked and waiting to be kindled.

"Before ye get him," Rory said, stopping Ewan. "I think it's best if we had a plan."

"Aye," Ewan agreed.

"Are ye certain he can be trusted?" Rory asked me.

I glanced at Shona who answered. "Yes. We've known him for as long as we can remember. He kept our trust safe from the meddling hands of our foster parents. He's helped us at every turning point in our lives. Well—" Shona paused for half a breath. "Most of them."

"It seems almost normal that he might have come to find us, to help us here," I said. "But I can't for the life of me figure out just how he would have gotten here, or how he would have known." I reached back with both hands, gathering my hair and twisting it into a knot at the nape of my neck. "It seems almost too uncanny that he might have met Emma and then magically appeared here."

"But, we have all done the same thing," Ewan said with a shrug.

"Honestly, at this point, I'm not certain I'd be wary of such," Rory said. "Think about it. What we did. What we've done. Where we've gone."

I nodded, but still, something in my gut didn't sit well, and one look at Shona said she felt the same way.

"I think we can trust him until he gives us a reason not to," I said.

"And be looking for that reason," Shona said. "He has been like a grandfather to us... But I was here for five years and didn't know who I was. Moira was home for years wondering if I was dead or alive. Why didn't he help then if he could?"

"I didn't think about it like that," I said. "But now that you mention it, why didn't he?"

"Let's ask him ourselves," Ewan said.

We waited for him to bring McAlister to the meeting room, and as soon as he did, I was struck with how much older our guardian appeared. His clothes were wrinkled and one pocket on his dark sport coat was torn. He was usually a lot more put together, but I suppose time travel could do that to a person.

"Lassies," Mr. McAlister drawled. He held out his arms to us, expecting us to rush to him, not something he'd ever done before which gave me pause.

Shona glanced at me; a look that was not hidden from anyone's view and we both stepped forward to embrace the man. Perhaps he was simply emotional from having time traveled. Goodness knows I was the same way.

Still, my guard was up. I couldn't put my finger on it, but something just wasn't right.

"Ye wouldn't' believe what has happened," he mumbled. "And, Shona, lass, ye look well. We were worried sick over your disappearance."

"What about Moira?" Shona asked, her eyes narrowed.

Mr. McAlister nodded. "When she went missing a few weeks ago, I gathered that it must have been time travel. Your neighbor said she'd seen the both of you with two men. I put two and two together, and came by your house each day on the off chance that ye returned."

"How have ye come to be here?" Rory asked, his arms crossed over his chest.

Mr. McAlister startled, glancing at Rory as if he'd only just seen him standing there. He frowned a moment and looked back at us.

"Does he... know?" Mr. McAlister asked us.

We both nodded and the man breathed a sigh of relief. His gaze was locked on the sideboard. "Can I beg a drink?"

Ewan grunted and went to pour a cup. He brought McAlister one then retreated to pour four more strong whiskies. I pretended to sip mine since I wasn't sure about a baby, and Shona shook her head, pushing the cup away.

"Ye didna answer my question," Rory said, eyeing McAlister over the rim of his cup.

McAlister choked on his whisky, and held his hand to his mouth, coughing. Nobody patted him on the back, all of us waiting for him to answer the question.

"Apologies for that, it went down the wrong pipe, it seems." Eyeing us all warily, he realized we weren't going to wait much longer to hear his story. Mr. McAlister sighed heavily, staring hard into his cup. "I've time traveled before. Many times. This is hard to explain." He looked up at us both, an apology in his eyes. "Ye see, I'm a time jumper. There are many of us. I can do it whenever I please."

I ground my teeth, trying to process what he said. He'd

practically just admitted that he could have come back in time, at any moment, to find Shona. To find myself. And he didn't.

"And yet you didn't help when Shona went missing years ago?" I asked.

"Before ye go jumping to conclusions, it's not as easy as it sounds. I have to know the exact place and time for it to work."

"You could have guessed. You could have gone many places," I said, feeling anger rise and burn in my chest.

"But I could have gone all over the world, thousands of times and never found her," he said.

"And how did ye end up here?" Rory asked, and I could tell his patience was wearing thin.

"The thing is," Mr. McAlister said, ignoring Rory. "I'm going to need ye to come home with me, lassies. It's not safe for ye here. There are other time jumpers, and if anyone were to find out who ye are, which I suspect they already know, then ye could be in mortal danger."

"We'll protect what is ours," Ewan said, standing beside Rory, the both of them looking like a couple of heathen warriors bent on murder. Their fingers were already wrapped around the hilts of their swords. Chests puffed. Teeth sufficiently bared. There was something very sexy in how protective my warrior was of me.

Mr. McAlister shrank back a little, but didn't change his tune.

He shook his head, hands fisted at his side. He stiffened, even his tallest height coming nowhere near the stature of the warriors. "I understand ye want to keep them, but they are not yours to keep."

"The hell they aren't," Rory roared. "They are our wives."

Before the argument could come to blows, I stepped forward.

"Mr. McAlister, my sister and I have often appreciated and followed your advice throughout our lives, but in this, I think I speak for the both of us when I say that we don't want to leave here. This is our home. We've made our lives here. We've married. We're starting families." I pointed to Shona's belly so as not to get Rory's hopes up about my own questionable condition. "If we were to leave, we'd need assurances we could come back."

"Aye, aye, of course. We'll come right back," he said.

"I don't believe you," Shona said, her voice soft but full of conviction. "You just said we had to leave because we are in mortal danger. You're only agreeing with Moira to get us to agree with you."

"Did ye see Emma?" Ewan asked. "Is that how ye knew to come here?"

Mr. McAlister's gaze shuttered, his eyes roving toward our feet. But that had to be the only reason, if he'd not known where we were before.

"Answer him," I demanded. "Did you see her?"

"Aye." He didn't expound on his answer.

I'd never felt the urge to shake an answer from someone more than I did at that moment.

"Where is she? How is she?" Ewan asked. "Is she the reason ye've come back?"

"She is fine." But his voice held a note I'd not heard before. A falsehood that, had I not known him my entire life, I might not have been able to pick up on so easily.

He was lying.

"She is not fine," I said. I fisted my hands at my side to keep from yanking on his torn jacket. "What has happened to her?"

"Ye're right." He met my gaze then. "And if ye dinna come with me, she might not ever be."

"Why? Who has her?" Ewan asked.

"I dinna know."

"How can ye not know?" Rory bellowed.

"Was Logan there?"

We fired question after question that went unanswered, and finally Mr. McAlister held up his hands.

"When I left... Her husband, Steven, had a gun to my head. And another barrel pressed to the head of the woman who brought Emma to your house. The woman who betrayed her."

I let out a gasp, my hands slapping to my mouth. "No!"

16

EMMA

I didn't know where I was going. And I'd never driven on the left side of the car, left side of the road before.

Vast expanses of highway passed us by. The city of Edinburgh disappeared into my rearview mirror and soon the view from the window was immense spans of dark wilderness. The shadows of trees, mountainsides, and the glow of the moon on the lochs.

The sun started to rise, purple in the distance, giving way to deep reds and orange, and the finally yellow, giving life to our surroundings. All in a myriad of colors. Green, red, yellow. Lush colors of autumn.

At first, I thought it was beautiful, and that it would be easier to navigate the roads to the Highlands, with the sun up, but that quickly changed. It was like I was learning to drive all over again. I was disoriented. Probably partly from the driving, but also because I was exhausted, hungry and I had to pee.

I felt bad for Logan who gripped tight to the seat as I swerved out of the right lane, nearing getting us both rocked by a semi-truck—and not for the first time since we'd gotten into the car.

"Love," Logan ground out. "Why do ye not pull this thing to a halt." He pointed at some woods a few dozen yards from the road, which also happened to be right next to a rest area. "We'll go into the forest and see if we can't figure out that black box."

"Okay, good idea. I need to make use of the facilities anyway," I murmured.

"I dinna know what that means, but I will follow ye."

I pulled the car over, wrenching on the parking break as I did so. I turned it off and started to climb out. Logan let out a long breath, patted my hand and smiled.

"I'd be verra happy never to ride in one of these things again."

I couldn't help laughing a little. "It wasn't fun for me, either."

"Glad I'm not the only one."

I showed him how to pull the lever to push open the door and he followed my actions. On the highway, one car after another whizzed past us. I walked to the women's side of the rest area, and Logan opted to wait outside. When I was done, he still stood there, completely on edge. I don't know why I'd been terrified that I'd come out and he'd be gone. But I was infinitely grateful to see that he was still there.

"Ready?" I asked.

"Never more." He leaned in, kissed my temple, and I pressed my hand to his heart, breathing in his scent and feeling calmer.

Hand in hand, we rushed across the asphalt of the parking lot until our feet hit the grass. A car honked behind us and Logan jumped.

"Just keep going." It was likely no one we knew, maybe someone cheering us on. From the looks of it, we might have been running off to the woods for quickie. No one knew we were actually running for our lives. And why would they have any reason to believe we were? Our story was completely our own. Our world was one in which fairytales were carved. Not the visualizations of reality.

As soon as we cleared the trees, we slowed to a stop, and I shivered with nerves and the fall chill. There was no time to grab a jacket and the thin black dress I wore was definitely not weather appropriate.

Logan searched our surrounding area, a habit I knew, and one that left me feeling safe. He seemed to have super human powers when it came to his senses. He could hear things, see things, and smell things well before I could.

"It appears no outlaws or Sassenachs are within the vicinity," he said.

I chewed my lip, trying to figure out the best way to tell him the woods now were a lot less scary then they were in 1544. "I don't think we have to worry about that so much now."

He raised a brow, frowning, a slow nod slightly bringing his chin down and up. "Right. I think ye mentioned something about Scotland and England uniting."

I nodded, wrapped my arms around his middle. "I know this is all so confusing and different for you."

"What about outlaws?"

"It's rare for them to live in the woods now, though you do find the occasional hermit, or serial killer."

Logan grunted. "So then we could still face dangers."

"Yes, but it is unlikely. The biggest worry I have is that if we were followed from Edinburgh, they will recognize Mrs. MacDonald's car and come searching for us. Mr. McAlister did put a tracker on the car and we were in such a hurry, I forgot to remove it. Maybe we should walk a bit further from the road, rather than contemplating the box here," I suggested. "Just in case anyone sees the car and comes looking."

"Good idea." Logan studied me, seeing me shiver and rub at my arms.

He unpinned his plaid from his shirt and tugged it over his head, revealing the ridges of his abdomen, his muscled chest, before passing it to me. "I dinna want ye to freeze afore we get to where we need to be."

I smiled and pushed it back, though I truly did want to pull its warmth over me. "Thank you, my darling, but I don't want you to freeze either."

He smiled and puffed his muscular chest, a sight that made my heart skip a beat. "I never freeze. Wear it, for me."

"All right." I pulled it on, grateful for the instant warmth. The shirt still held some of his heat, all of his intoxicating earthy-spicy scent. The fabric swarmed around me, coming to just below my knees. The arms were easily six inches past my hands, so I rolled them up. "I am very warm now."

"I am pleased." Logan held out his hand to me. Once I'd slipped my hand against his larger, coarser palm, he scanned the woods. "Any idea where to?"

I shook my head. "I don't think it will matter. Maybe a mile or so?"

We walked for about fifteen minutes, Logan keeping pace with my smaller strides. I was thankful that at Gealach I'd ignored his edicts to stay in bed after having the baby, or else I wouldn't have had the stamina I needed now to walk quickly and far, while being extremely exhausted.

We stopped in a natural clearing with a large flat stone, warmed from the sun that shone through the bare trees. I sat down, trying to soak up the warmth.

Logan sat beside me, wrapping his arm around my shoulder and pulling me close. I leaned my head on him, absorbing some of his strength and heat.

He kissed my forehead and then my lips, a languid, loving kiss.

We stayed like that for several heartbeats. Just the two of us, quiet and peaceful, one with nature. Funny how this part of the woods, so far from any sort of technology or modern life, could have been any time.

We changed, what we could do transformed, but the world around us, it stayed the same. Tranquil, wild beauty.

Logan whispered. "Let's try to go home."

I nodded, pulling the black box from my purse with trembling fingers.

There was a small latch on the front, and when I opened it, it looked a little like a miniature, but thick, laptop. Almost like one of those handheld games from my youth. There was a screen, a power button, a keyboard, and a red button, that like in all movies, I assumed was the emergency "don't ever press this," button.

I studied the small computer. A time jumper's key to any period within all our history. What about the future? Did it have to be a time that had already passed? This small box, seemingly insignificant, was actually a tool that if it got into the wrong hands could change the course of history for good or bad. Terrifying, really.

Blowing out a breath that was harsh enough to make my hair flutter around my face, I pushed the power button and the machine whirred to life.

But then there was nothing, just a blinking cursor on a blank, blue screen. Obviously a protective measure should it be stolen. There had to be some sort of code. Or could it truly be as simple as typing in where a person wanted to go?

"What do ye do?" Logan asked.

I shook my head. "I don't know. Hold onto me. I'm going to try a few things and I want to make sure if any of them work, we are not separated."

"Do ye think it is as simple as that?"

"I don't know, but it seems so. I mean, if couples can time travel by making love? It has to be touch, right?"

Logan shook his head, looking just as perplexed as myself. "I dinna know. But if I had to make a guess, then aye."

"All right." I blew out another breath, my heart pounding hard. "Here I go."

Logan wrapped his arms around my middle, his chin resting on my shoulder.

I typed in *1544* then pressed the return button. Freezing. I didn't know what to expect. But I didn't feel any different. There was no shift in the wind. In fact, nothing happened, and the 1544 disappeared from the screen.

"Okay, that didn't work," I mumbled. "Let me try to be more specific."

I typed in *Gealach, 1544* and pressed enter. Again, nothing happened.

"Dammit," I muttered, so frustrated. I gritted my teeth. Tore my gaze from the screen to stare at the sky for a minute.

What had Mrs. MacDonald said? *Punch in where you want to go.* I'd done that. My eye lit on the red button. Maybe *that* was *the* button. Not an emergency, don't press it button, but the one that made you disappear.

"Breathe, love. We'll figure it out," Logan murmured, massaging my shoulders.

"I'm going to try something different," I said.

"All right."

"Put your arms around me again, and don't let go. No matter what, hold on tight," I said.

This time, I typed, *Castle Gealach, July, 1544.* My finger hesitated over the red button, scared to press it and not have it work, but equally terrified that it would and one of us wouldn't end up going. I settled the black box on my knees, and with my free hand threaded my fingers through Logan's where his palm rested around my waist.

"I love you," I said, touching my temple to his.

"I love ye, too."

I bit my lip hard, still unable to make my finger move.

"Press it," he whispered.

And I did.

Reality pulsed in an out around me, like it had the first time I'd time traveled. I heard noises that were different, and then nothing. The air turned warm, then frigid. Through it all, I held tight to Logan—and the black box, the logical part of me realizing if we ended up somewhere else, not where we wanted to be, we'd need that thing to get back. We'd been given an enchanted prize, and we needed to keep it safe. No matter what. We couldn't allow it to get back into Mrs. MacDonald's wretched hands.

Beside me, Logan groaned.

"I think it's working," I said, my voice sounding so far away, like I wasn't the one who'd said it.

"Aye. I feel queasy."

The dawn bloomed into a bright sun, then faded, and then brightened again.

I felt woozy, and as though my limbs were being pulled in forty different directions.

"Stay with me," I heard Logan say, his voice echoing remotely, though his arms were still locked tight around me.

"Always," I shouted, wanting to hear my voice louder than the pounding of the earth as it shifted this way and that.

But shouting didn't help. I still sounded far away. I wanted to close my eyes, to hide from view the way the world pulsed in and out around me, but I couldn't. I didn't want to lose sight of Logan's hand twined with mine.

A moment later, the atmosphere sucked in on itself, turning black. I blinked, screamed. I couldn't see anything.

Like we'd been forced into a void. Logan's breath pounded against my ear, and then, just as suddenly, the world was light again.

We sat in what looked to be the very same clearing.

"It didn't work," I said.

"Or it did." Logan stood on shaky legs and held out his hands to me. "We won't know for certain until we go back toward the road."

"You're right."

"Nature is nature. The same as it's always been for hundreds of years." He pulled me up and I tucked the black box back into my purse. "For one thing," he said. "It is a hell of a lot warmer here."

"Then it must have worked." Heat touched my face. "It was summer when we left Gealach." I held out my hands. "This feels like summer."

I pulled off his *leine,* handing it back and watched him pull it on, pinning his plaid in place. A twinge of disappointment passed through me at his having to cover himself. I certainly had enjoyed the view, and the touch of his bare skin. Soon enough, we'd be back at our castle, and once I'd gotten to snuggle with Saor, I was going to lock Logan up in our chamber for a month or more.

We walked in silence, each of us listening to the sounds of summer. We'd definitely traveled away from November in Scotland, though it would have helped to know exactly where I'd pulled off the side of the road. I wasn't sure if I'd gone north, south, east or west. I didn't even know how long I'd driven. We were either near Gealach, as I'd punched into the computer, or we were wherever it was that I'd pulled off at the rest stop. We could have been near the border of England or the Highlands. And frustratingly, there was no way to know just yet.

"I'm sorry for not paying better attention to where we

were," I muttered. An idea occurred to me, and I pulled Mrs. MacDonald's cell phone from the purse. But it was dead. Not even a flicker of battery life. I could have sworn it was at least fifty percent charged when I'd taken it from the old bat. That was a good sign. "No cell towers."

Logan gave me an odd look. I shoved the cell phone back into the purse.

"No need to worry on that account, lass. Wherever we are, we'll figure it out. Soon we'll be back at Gealach with our son and our friends."

I nodded, though I had doubts that were doing a good job of trying to creep into my thoughts. A sudden shiver took hold as my nerves threatened to undo me. Now was not the time to panic. I could panic later.

But still my thoughts came through loud and clear.

Would Mrs. MacDonald follow us? After she got her wound taken care of? As a time jumper, she probably had access to more black boxes. And where was McAlister? And Steven?

So many questions and no way to get the answers.

"What was that?" Logan hissed.

He put his arms out to protect me, standing stock still, his eyes wide, head cocked to the side as he listened to something I couldn't hear.

I didn't make a noise, didn't even breathe for fear of making a sound that would interfere with him deciphering whatever it was that he'd heard.

"We're being followed," he said under his breath. "Pretend as though ye did not hear anything."

I didn't hear anything, so that was easy. What wasn't easy, was *knowing* we were being followed, and all the other questionable variables that came with it, and pretending as though I had no idea. Man or animal? Friend or foe? One or many?

Did they want to rob us or murder us? Was it Steven? MacDonald? McAlister?

Logan sped up a little bit at a time, so the increased pace was not as noticeable.

"Halt, you bloody Scot!"

"Sassenachs," Logan hissed, whipping around, and keeping me at his back.

Oh, dear god! We'd definitely traveled back in time, and landed into the very hands of the English!

"Run," he ground out to me when they weren't just behind him.

Holding my hand tight, he started to run and I worked hard to keep up, but his legs were long and I was tired. I tripped several times before he swung me up into his arms and kept on running as though the added weight were nothing to him.

"Get back here, you heathen!"

The voice was the same, but the sound of the crashing from behind us had the distinct sound of more than one man.

"How many do you think?" I asked, clinging to Logan as he ran.

"At least six."

That was too many for him to fight off alone, and while he'd taught me self-defense, I wasn't exactly a warrior by any stretch of the imagination.

Where had the black box taken us? The woods of Gealach had often been filled with English, but not as of late...

With eyes wide open, I prayed we weren't caught.

17

LOGAN

Less than a quarter hour later, I set Emma down beside a small spring with a waterfall at its back. A gentle spray misted the morning air. The sound of the falls as it spilled over the top of a crest some fifty feet in the air was thunderous. Dangerous, in that I couldn't hear our enemy approach from afar, but safe, because they couldn't hear us, either.

Emma shook, though the air was warm, and dipped her hands in the water, bringing them cupped to her lips.

"We've lost them for now," I said.

"Do you recognize this spring?" she asked, studying the green foliage around us.

Small flowers dotted the landscape, and just above the spring, the sun shone down, warming the spot. It was tranquil, a location I recalled stopping to water horses and rest some years before. I'd not explored it greatly then, too much in a hurry to return to my castle.

I nodded. "I think we are on the perimeter of Gealach lands. At least a day or two's walk to get back to the castle. If we had a horse, we could be there by nightfall."

Emma rubbed water on the back of her neck. "Maybe we'll pass a village along the way that will give us horses. You are their laird, a good and just leader. I think they'd be happy to help you."

Her faith in me never ceased to amaze. "Aye, but if they were to do so, and the English are following, it will only put my people in danger. I dinna want to lead them to a village's gates."

"Surely a scout has spotted the English and gotten word back to Ewan." She took another sip of water, the color that had faded from her skin when I first found her was returning, and the bruise on her cheek seemed to have miraculously also faded to a yellow, as though it happened a much longer time ago than just the night before. "Will he not assemble warriors to meet the English upon their way?"

She had a good point. I grinned, proud of her for taking on the role of Lady of Gealach with such spark. "Aye. If one of the local garrison's has not already been warned. I keep men, fully armed, at various spots throughout our land."

"Then perhaps, we should head toward them?" Emma asked. Her lips trembled with a fear she was trying to hide.

A part of my ego was wounded that she didn't feel safe just being with me, but I was also not a complete fool. We'd just had to run from six *Sassenachs* who would have killed me and tormented her.

"Aye," I lied, wanting to ease her fears.

I couldn't tell her the truth—that the English were most likely headed straight for those outposts, and the worst place for us to go would be toward my scattered forts.

Aye, they had walls and numbers that could protect us—if we made it. Having men, weapons and horses at our back would give us an advantage, but I wasn't willing to put my wife in danger by deliberately setting her upon the English's path. If we didn't make it before the English arrived there, we were dead. If they happened to ambush us on the road, we were dead. It was too risky. I'd already lost her once; I simply couldn't chance losing her again.

The one advantage we did have now was that the English didn't know these lands like I did. The best decision would be for us to hide for the rest of the day, and when night fell, make our move. The English would not be brave enough to travel at night. And if they were, they wouldn't be as prepared as I was, nor as easily able to hide with their larger numbers, not to mention, I could hear their chainmail and armor clinking a mile away. At least, I could before we arrived at the waterfall.

I squatted beside Emma and dipped my hands into the water, wishing I had a water skin to fill to keep us hydrated. We had no food, either. I frowned. It was going to be a long day if we didn't have *something* to eat.

Around the waterfall, there were often berry bushes and even the occasional nut tree. I couldn't risk hunting and lighting a fire to cook our food.

"Let us forage, before we go into hiding," I suggested.

"Where will we hide?" Her eyes scanned the area.

"A cave, perhaps," I murmured, looking up toward the mouth of the waterfall. Where there were mountains, there was always a cave, one just had to look—and evict any animal that had taken up residence.

"What about behind the waterfall?" Emma suggested.

I glanced at the falls, the darkness that seeped from behind the curtains of water. The water fell hard in yards of thick ribbons. I couldn't see behind the waves enough to determine if there was a ledge. "'Tis a possibility. I'll examine it closer."

I walked as near as I could around the perimeter of the spring, getting close to the side of the mountain, and still, peering around what I thought to be the edge of the falls, I couldn't tell if there was an opening behind it or not. "I'll have to swim over."

"Okay," Emma said, her teeth chattering.

Och, but I loathed the fear that filled her. I wanted to take it away, to destroy it, but I knew the only way to do that was to get her to safety, or to distract her at least.

I disrobed, turning to wink at her, as I stood naked in the sun. That was enough to get her teeth to cease their chattering for a minute. A sultry smile curled her lush lips and she batted her lashes at me, before raking her gaze hotly over my figure. Instantly, I was hard, filled with need and wanting. I dove into the water, letting the chill calm my heated body. A few strokes and I came up near the falls, with my *sgian dubh* drawn, in case there was some creature that had made a residence of the very place we wished to hide.

Being that there was no obvious opening between the water and the side of the mountain, I was mostly convinced that the droves simply fell against the side of the ridge, but when I thrust my hand through the water, I felt only air. Moving my hand down I met a flat ledge.

I thrust my head through the torrents, blinking away the water from my eyes. There was, indeed, a cave, damp and dark, completely hidden from view. It didn't go back far, maybe five feet at the most, and it was only eight or so feet wide. Plenty of space for us to hide for a time. There didn't appear to be any creatures there now, nor did it smell as though any had been there for some time.

I came back through the water and turned to face my wife, taking in her expectant and worried gaze. I nodded, not wanting to shout over the falls and not even certain if she'd hear me if I did.

Emma's face brightened.

I waved for her to jump in.

She stood, untied her robe-like gown at her waist,

standing in only her undergarment. The sun shone on her full breasts, showing how perfectly creamy her skin was. She shoved the gown into her bag and held the satchel over her head. She dipped her toes into the chilly spring, and then leapt back with a tiny shriek, shrinking away from the water's edge as though she'd stepped on ice.

I laughed and swam toward her until I was standing, towering, over my petite, fireball of a wife.

"I'll carry ye," I said.

"I can swim."

"I know ye can." I winked. "But I like touching ye."

She wrapped her arms around my neck and I lifted her effortlessly. Her silky skin smoothed over mine, and it was hard not to crush her to me. To forget about the English trolling the woods and make love to her beneath the light of the sun.

"What about your things?" she asked.

"I'll come back to fetch them. I wanted to check for berries and nuts. Get us something to eat."

"I grabbed a couple of power bars from the kitchen at Moira's," she said. "So we can eat."

"Power bar?" I asked, wiggling my brows. "Will it give me special powers?"

Emma laughed. "Maybe. What kind of powers do you want?"

We moved through the water, her gasping as the chilled depths touched her rear, and rose up to her waist. I clutched her closer.

"I would have the power for a stamina that never ceased," I said, nipping her ear.

Emma's head fell back, and she let out a laugh that I wished hadn't been dulled by the roaring of the waterfall.

"Do ye approve, wife?" I teased.

She leaned forward, pressing her forehead to mine and

kissed me gently. "Any more stamina and you just might kill me," she teased.

I chuckled. "Ye'd die of pleasure, is there a better way to go?"

"None," she agreed.

We made it to the fall's base. "Are ye ready? I'm going to thrust ye through, and then fetch my things."

Emma glanced up, her gaze riveted on the tallest point of the rise where the water spilled over. Droplets landed delicately on her cheeks and I longed to lick them away. "As ready as I'll ever be."

I let her catch her breath and then pushed her through. Emma let out another squeal that was swallowed by the roar of the falls. I called an apology, though I wasn't certain she'd heard it.

I hurried back to the side, grabbing hold of my clothes, when I caught the sound of metal chinking. *Ballocks*. We'd not lost the bloody *Sassenachs* fast enough. And if I could hear them through the pounding of the falls, they were close. Closer than I liked. A chill snaked up my spine. They could break through the brush before I had a chance to get back to the cave. But if I didn't get back, Emma would worry, she might poke her head out, be seen by the enemy, and then it would be over. All this went through my mind in less than a second, before I was acting.

Mo chreach!

I balled up my clothes and shoved them under one arm, racing back to the fall's base. Checking one last time for anyone coming through the brush, and seeing no one, I shoved myself through the cascade.

I rolled to a landing at my wife's knees where she sat, already re-clothed—a fact that I found slightly disappointing. No matter, I could always remove them again.

I held my fingers to my lips, and then pointed toward where we'd just come from.

Emma's mouth fell open and she held the back of her hand to her teeth. Pulling her hand away from her face, she mouthed, *the English*?

I nodded, and kissed that hand.

I spread out my plaid, dry at the center, on the ground, donned my *leine*, and pulled her to me.

Emma shivered, and clutched to me.

We remained still, silent, for many minutes. Could have been even half an hour. Emma pulled out the things she'd called power bars, their flavors strong, sweet, and leaving a film on my mouth that was most unpleasant. Carefully, I skimmed some water from the falls, certain no one could see me from the outside, and offered a drink to my wife. Once she was satisfied, I rinsed my mouth. The power bars might have tasted odd, but they were filling.

So far, there were no signs of the English coming close to the falls, though I wasn't going to risk looking. Every once in awhile, I could hear the sounds of metal chinking. They were still searching the area. All I could do was pray that they didn't think to look behind the falls. My sword was drawn, and at my side. I was prepared to drive its sharpened tip through anyone who dared come near to us.

The spray of the water, and the darkened space, was colder than the temperature of the summer sun. If my plaid had not been soaked, I'd have wrapped it around Emma who shivered from fear and a genuine chill.

Since we'd be here for hours more until the sun fell, I knew of another way we could pass the time... One that would keep us both warm, and distract Emma away from her fear.

I nuzzled her cheek, gently pressing my fingers to her chin until she turned to kiss me. She was stiff in my embrace, but with a few swipes of my tongue against hers, she loosened, until she wrapped her arms around my shoulders and held on tight.

"Emma," I breathed against her ear, using my teeth to scrape against her earlobe.

She clung closer, and I lifted her onto my lap, scooting back until my spine hit stone. I kissed her, caressed her, teased her skin until she prickled with pleasure, the chills of cold gone, replaced by a heat that built and built. Her soft sighs and urgent moans spurned my own heated desire.

Emma moved to straddle me, lifting her gown and my shirt out of the way, our lower bodies colliding, nude.

Pressing her hands to the side of my face, she leaned low and whispered against my ear. "You do know the perfect way to distract me."

"So I am not as clever as I thought?"

"Oh, no, my love, you are very clever. And sexy, handsome, powerful, cunning, protective. I could not have married a better man."

"Och, to hear ye say those things love, ye'll make my head grow big, my ego even bigger."

"'Tis not bad to stroke your ego," she said, reaching her hand between us. "Especially if it is while I am stroking your cock."

I groaned, trying to keep the sound soft so as not to overpower the thunder of the falls. Her hand was magic, silky, smooth, and she knew just the right way to touch me.

"I canna be the only one..." I murmured, sliding my hands up her thighs, my fingers dipping against her moist sex.

She shivered, and I swallowed her cries of pleasure with a searing kiss that left us both craving more.

Unable to take the separation any longer, I tugged her hips forward, sliding my cock along the seam of her nether-lips until I reached her entrance.

Emma rocked forward at the same time I thrust, driving all the way up inside her. Her cunny, slick and hot, gripped me, stroked me.

"Och, my love," I murmured, biting her lower lip and sucking. "I'm so glad I found ye."

"Me, too. Me, too..." She kissed me hard then, tightening her hold on me, driving her hands through my hair and tugging hard at the base of my skull.

Tendrils of pleasure radiated through my body. I loved the way she touched me, claimed me as her own, even as I did the same.

Emma rocked back and forth on top of me, her knees settled beside me, and then she was riding me in earnest, set on finding release. I held tight to her hips, hissed a breath and forced myself not to climax right then and there. It was hard not to lose complete control when my wife took over the pace. Any sense of control was loose and slippery in my grasp, and I stopped fighting it. Stopped trying to grasp hold, and instead, I rode the waves of her pleasure, kissing and swallowing every sensual moan.

🦢 18 🦢

EMMA

When I woke on the chill, damp cave floor, it was to Logan's whispered words against my cheek. "We need to go now."

His arms were still around me, my back flush to his chest. We'd slept for hours. I couldn't be sure just how long, but the sun had set, and the cave was nearly pitch black except for the silver-hued shards of water falling.

I nodded, rolling in his arms and clutching him to me. One more embrace before we were once more running for our lives.

"Fold your gown up into your satchel again," he said. "Else, ye'll be draped in cold water the whole night through and without the sun, ye'll not be able to get warm quick enough."

I started to undress, goose bumps skating over my arms and legs. I was grateful for the heat, which always seemed to radiate from his skin.

The moon shone on the surface of the water, making it sparkle black and gold. We slipped in, unseen, and even though I was prepared for the bite of its chill, I still had to grit my teeth. The water came up to my waist.

Neither of us said a word as we crossed to the left side of the shore. The water didn't get shallower as it did on the far side, but stayed at about waist level. The floor of the spring was covered in slippery stones and moss. I tiptoed carefully, not wanting to slip and make a splash.

Logan tried to tug me into his arms, but I thought I might actually be warmer using my own muscles to pull my weight through the water. But, since it wasn't too far of a distance, I didn't end up exerting enough energy to make a difference. Logan paused at the shore, his hands flattened to the bank. I stilled. He pointed to his ear, to let me know he was trying to listen for any unusual sounds before getting out.

Not hearing anything, he nodded and then wrapped his hands around my waist and lifted me effortlessly onto the bank. Then, he all but leapt from the water, landing on his feet beside me.

Shivering, I clamped my jaw tight, to keep my teeth from chattering. I pulled out my dry gown and put it back on, the cotton fabric soaking up the water on my skin and my under-wear. I'd gone without a bra... Big mistake as it would have kept me warmer. Then again, it would have been soaked right now. So, maybe it was better that I'd left it at Moira and Shona's house.

Logan's plaid, which had dried through the hours we'd spent in the cave, seemed to have remained so. He'd balled it up once more, tucking it close to his body as he leapt through the falls. He'd held it over his head as he crossed the small pool, not letting it touch. I eyed it with envy, but didn't dare ask for his clothing.

"Love," Logan said, and I glanced at him. He was gazing down at me, the corner of his lip turned up in a grin. "Put this on, at least for a little while, will ye? Judging from where we are, there is a village close by that we can pilfer a few items, unseen, to make the journey home."

"I can't take your clothes," I argued.

He held out his arms. "I'm wearing my shirt. Just for a little bit, until ye feel warm enough to share it."

"All right. But only for a little bit." As he passed it to me, I kissed the back of his hand. "Thank you."

I wrapped his plaid around me, only mildly damp at the edges; it held a heat to it that my simple dress did not.

"Anything for ye, love." He stroked my spine, and hugged me close for several heartbeats, rubbing warmth back into my bones.

We started to walk, a brisk pace, me taking at least two steps for every stride of Logan's. I started to warm up quickly, even had a tiny prickle of sweat on my upper lip.

About an hour or so later, the flat lands to our right rose up in unnatural square and triangular shapes. A village.

I shoved Logan's plaid at him and whispered, "Just in case. I don't want you to be confronted without a plaid on. They'll think you're a miscreant of some sort, not recognizing you as their laird."

Logan let out a soft chuckle. "Wouldn't that be a story for the ages? Their laird sneaking into their village, practically nude, to steal from them?"

I laughed, and then bit my lip to silence myself. We'd not seen or heard any English since leaving the falls, nor any Scotsman—outlaw or no. We'd been pretty darn lucky actually, since leaving, and I prayed it remained so. Of all people, we deserved to have a bit of luck on our side.

"Stay close." Fully dressed, Logan crept forward, bent slightly at the waist, and I did the same, not wanting to take a chance of being noticed.

A remote village like this would have at least one sentry

on duty. About a hundred yards from the settlement, Logan dropped to his knees tugging me down.

He pointed toward the gated entrance—indeed, up on a small platform at the top of their wooden wall was a guard.

Logan made a circular motion with his hand, and I got the impression he wanted to approach the village from the rear. Keeping ourselves crouched low, we half-walked, half-ran, two hunchbacks stealing through the night of their own lands.

At the back of the village, Logan peered through the slats of the postern gate. There wasn't anyone there. Our luck did, indeed, appear to be improving.

"Stay here," he said.

I nodded, ducking to a crouch.

Logan disappeared into the village. My eyes were wide, staring into the wide expanse of the dark that surrounded the small parish, wishing there had been just an ounce of battery juice left in Mrs. MacDonald's phone so I could put the flashlight on... just in case I needed to see something.

To keep myself calm, I started to count. *One. Two. Three. Four. Five... Fifty-seven. Fifty-eight. Fifty-nine.* All the way to one hundred, and still no sign of him.

I rubbed my eyes, to wipe away the sting of holding them open for so long.

"Come on, Logan," I whispered. "Get back out here."

My prayers were answered a few moments later when Logan emerged, the hot breath of a mount fanning over my face. I gazed up into the fuzzy, flared nostrils of a large horse. Logan reached down, and in one fluid motion, I grabbed onto his arm and he swung me up into the saddle in front of him. He wrapped me in a clean, warm, dry plaid, and I had to bite my lip to keep from moaning aloud at the feeling of warmth.

"We'll be there much sooner, now," he whispered against my ear. "Ye'll be able to hold your bairn again before daybreak, with luck."

I smiled up at him. "I can't wait."

Logan nuzzled my neck. "I know Saor has been missing ye."

He walked the mount a fair distance away so as not to alert the one guard with the pounding of hooves. Once we were well enough away, he urged the horse into a gallop. I snuggled closer to him, holding on and filled with hope, elation, and relief.

This nightmare was soon going to be at an end. At home, finally, and reunited with my child. There was still of course the issue of Steven, Mrs. MacDonald and McAlister, but they could wait. I just wanted to be in my own bed, surrounded by the ones I loved.

A few hours later, just as Logan promised, before the sun had risen, we descended the mountain and Gealach's towers, lit by torches, came into view.

"We're home," Logan said, his tone filled with the same sense of relief I felt. He urged the mount into a faster gallop and we charged down the mountainside, sailing over the heath toward the gates. "Cover your ears."

I did as he suggested, pressing my hands to the side of my head.

Logan bellowed for the guards to raise the portcullis, to open the gates, in the name of their laird and mistress.

There was a great clambering of men on the battlements, of people rushing to do Logan's bidding, combined with cheers, and shouts that echoed into the moonlit night.

As soon as we were through the gates, Shona ran at me, Saor in her arms.

I gasped, nearly choking on it as I reached for my child. Logan was quick to set me down from the horse, before I fell off in my eagerness to hold my baby again.

I wrapped my arms around him, pressed my lips to his head. Tears stung my eyes as I met his bright blue gaze. A smile touched his perfect little mouth and he wiggled and cooed with excitement in my arms.

Shona and Ewan embraced me with Saor in my arms, both loudly proclaiming their pleasure at my return.

"Where are Moira and Rory?" Logan asked.

"Bad news," Ewan said. "A missive arrived from Dunleod. Ranulf, Rory's son, the one who he'd had to lock up on account of his wanting his father dead?"

Logan nodded recognition. I barely listened, too enamored with the motherly love coursing through my veins.

"He's escaped. Moira and Rory rushed back to Dunleod to assemble a search party. They fear Ranulf will put himself in danger in his eagerness to see revenge done on his father and his clan who abandoned him."

That did get my attention. Ranulf hated Moira. Had threatened both their lives.

Wee Saor wrapped his chubby fingers around mine and held on tight, gurgling his pleasure.

"I do not envy them the task ahead." Logan shook his head.

I clutched my baby to my chest, once more, my nose buried in his tuft of hair, smelling that sweet, soft scent. I could have breathed him in all day.

Saor cooed and gurgled, grasping at my skin. He smiled a wide, gummy grin, and I smiled back, rubbing my nose against his.

"There is something else, my laird," Ewan said. "A visitor."

"Who is it?" Logan's voice was filled with irritation.

I knew he wanted to get up to our private chamber as much as I did, to be alone, just the three of us. A visitor was throwing a wrench in our plans for peace.

"A man named McAlister."

I gasped, clutching Saor tighter to me. "Is he in the dungeon?" I asked.

Ewan looked startled, as did Shona beside me.

"Ye met him?" Shona asked.

"Aye." I stiffened, suddenly on edge, recalling the sneaky older man. "He is not to be trusted."

"Escort him to the dungeon," Logan ordered, taking in my stricken expression.

Ewan touched the hilt of his sword. "Right away my laird."

"Wait, before you go," I asked. "Did he say why he was here?"

"He wanted to take Moira and I away," Shona explained. "For our safety. Though he didn't expound on it, even when pressed. The man was quite jittery, and after relaying that he believed Steven had you in captivity, he asked to retire. We've not yet had a chance to speak with him further."

I nodded. "I do not fully understand everything myself, but there are a lot more people that can time travel, that *are* time traveling, of their own volition."

I glanced around the courtyard, suddenly realizing we were not alone. Luckily it did not appear that anyone had heard what I said.

Logan put his arm around my shoulders. "Let's retreat to the library."

"I'll meet ye there," Ewan said. "I'll have the man escorted to a more secure location, while we try to figure out what is going on."

"I think that's best," Logan said.

Shona still looked extremely concerned.

We hurried to the library, the nursemaid, attempting to take Saor from me, but I shook my head. I'd not been able to nurse my baby in two days. I didn't care who saw, I was going to do it.

In the library, I tucked Saor beneath the plaid, and he

eagerly latched on. I sighed with relief, the painful pressure I'd been ignoring finally waning.

I listened as Ewan explained McAlister's visit. I filled in what had happened to me with Steven, Mrs. MacDonald and McAlister before Logan appeared, and then Logan relayed what had happened when he arrived at Shona and Moira's house.

"And that is why we cannot trust McAlister. We don't know whose side he's on or what his agenda is," I said.

"I agree. There are too many questions he wasn't able to —or refused to—answer," Shona pointed out. "I have a suspicion he wants to take Shona and I back in time, to have us claim our rightful place as rulers. We don't want to do that."

"Logan and I will support whatever you decide," I said, glancing up at my husband and sharing a secret smile. "We certainly can understand rejecting the crown, even if it is yours to take."

"As ye had before, ye have my protection, and whatever ye need."

"There is more," I whispered. "Mrs. MacDonald is surely going to try to find us. She knows where we are. And she has probably already had contact with the MacDonalds who want Logan dead."

"And what about Steven?" Ewan asked, his hands fisting at his sides.

"He wants my wife back." Logan's tone was filled with fury. "But he's not going to get her."

"He is a time jumper," I said. "There is a possibility he will end up here. And since he'd already partnered with Mrs. MacDonald before, I wouldn't be surprised if they both partnered up again."

"We cannot let McAlister go. If he were to be set free and decided to also form a bond... Three time jumpers in one group against us." Logan shook his head. "Those odds are not good."

With Saor satisfied, I burped him and then passed him to Logan who held out his arms. I felt a twinge of sadness with him no longer against me, but at least he was with his father, that was a good feeling. A whimsical smile came to my lips. I loved to watch Logan cuddle Saor. This huge, muscular warrior, easily twenty times the size of our baby, a practical giant... It was adorable.

Shaking myself back to the present, I pulled out the black box.

"This is what brought us back here." I gazed at them all, seriously. "This is the tool that the time jumpers have at their disposal. The ability to go anywhere, anytime they choose. And they can take people with them. This is what Fate has been fighting. They each have one and we have only this single box between the six of us."

"And this is why I think Fate pulled Emma forward in time. She needed her to find this out. To get her hands on one of these tools. I've been the guardian of Scotland's secrets for a long time. We are now all going to take on the task of being the guardians of time, if ye're willing that is," Logan said, his gaze just as serious as mine.

"Count me in," Ewan said, nodding, his eyes locked on me, then to his own wife.

"Without a doubt," Shona agreed. "Moira and Rory will agree. I feel comfortable speaking for them in saying they will join us."

"I am with you always," I said.

Logan nodded then pulled me into his embrace, with Saor between the two of us.

"Together, we will save Scotland. No longer are we Highland bound, we are the keepers of time."

While this may be *The End* for now—'tis not truly over... Look for the next installments of the Highland Bound series:

Draped in Plaid

WANT MORE SEXY TIME-TRAVELING HIGHLANDERS? CHECK out my Touchstone novella series!

Highland Steam
Highland Brawn
Highland Tryst
Highland Heat

If you enjoyed **HIGHLANDER UNDONE**, *please spread the word by leaving a review on the site where you purchased your copy, or a reader site such as Goodreads! I love to hear from readers! Visit me on Facebook:* https://www.facebook.com/elizaknightfiction. I'm also on Instagram @ElizaKnightFiction and Twitter: @ElizaKnight *Many thanks!*

Stay tuned for Summer 2021 and Eliza's brand new Scottish Regency series — SCOTS OF HONOR!

Highland war heroes rebuilding their lives grapple with ladies forging their own paths—who will win?

Regency Scotland comes alive in the vibrant and sexy new SCOTS OF HONOR series by USA Today bestselling author Eliza Knight. Scottish military heroes, who want nothing more than to lay low after the ravages of war in 19th century France, find their Highland homecomings vastly contradict their simple desires. Especially when they meet the feisty lasses who are tenacious enough to take them on, and show them just what they've been missing out of life. In battle they can't be beaten, but in love, they all find the ultimate surrender.

Return of the Scot
The Scot is Hers
Taming the Scot

WANT TO READ MORE SCOTTISH ROMANCE NOVELS BY ELIZA? CHECK OUT HER STOLEN BRIDE SERIES!

The Highlander's Temptation
The Highlander's Reward
The Highlander's Conquest
The Highlander's Lady
The Highlander's Warrior Bride
The Highlander's Triumph
The Highlander's Sin
Wild Highland Mistletoe (a Stolen Bride winter novella)
The Highlander's Charm (a Stolen Bride novella)
A Kilted Christmas Wish – a contemporary Holiday spin-off
The Highlander's Surrender
The Highlander's Dare

ABOUT THE AUTHOR

Eliza Knight is an award-winning and *USA Today* bestselling author of over fifty sizzling historical romance and erotic romance. Under the name E. Knight, she pens rip-your-heart-out historical fiction. While not reading, writing or researching for her latest book, she chases after her three children. In her spare time (if there is such a thing...) she likes daydreaming, wine-tasting, traveling, hiking, staring at the stars, watching movies, shopping and visiting with family and friends. She lives atop a small mountain with her own knight in shining armor, three princesses and two very naughty puppies. Visit Eliza at http://www.elizaknight.com or her historical blog History Undressed: www.historyun-dressed.com. Sign up for her newsletter to get news about books, events, contests and sneak peaks! http://eepurl.com/CSFFD

Made in the USA
Monee, IL
10 April 2021

65294664R00115